Dear Megan,

Surprise, surprise! I know it's kind of a shock, but as you can see, I never filed your marriage license. This is kind of hard to explain, but here goes.

I got pretty drunk at your wedding reception, remember?
(Oh, yes, he certainly had. Megan also remembered that Reed's dark disapproval of their best man's behavior had taken some of her joy out of the day.)

Every time I saw Reed I had another drink. I ended up not filing the license out of sheer spite. After I sobered up, I decided to call my lawyer. According to him, you have one year to file a marriage license—and until it's filed, you're not legally married.
(Good Lord, she wasn't married, after all!)

I'm glad I did it, Meggie. Reed Kendall will never give you a divorce. So I'm sending you your ticket to freedom. Burn this license and you're home free. Keep it, file it with city hall, and you'll end up an unhappy bitter woman—if you aren't already.
(She wasn't bitter, she told herself. She wasn't. And she did love her husband. But she was unhappy, desperately so.)

Your anniversary is in six weeks. You have that long to decide. It's your choice.

Love,

Jerry

Anne Marie Duquette has traveled extensively throughout the United States, first as an air force "brat" and then as a member of the military herself. She started her writing career as a young girl, with lengthy letters to relatives and friends describing her impressions of countless new duty locations. Now married to a career naval officer and the mother of two young children, she still likes to travel—though with a family and a successful writing career, she finds less time for it!

Anne Marie has published six Harlequin Romance novels, including the recent *On the Line,* which was featured in the series' Back to the Ranch promotion. Her first American Romance title was also published last year as one of four "Superheroes" stories.

Dedicated to Mara Villotti,
who had the courage
to begin again.

ANNIVERSARY WALTZ

Anne Marie Duquette

W✪RLDWIDE®

TORONTO • NEW YORK • LONDON
AMSTERDAM • PARIS • SYDNEY • HAMBURG
STOCKHOLM • ATHENS • TOKYO • MILAN
MADRID • WARSAW • BUDAPEST • AUCKLAND

Special thanks and acknowledgment to
Anne Marie Duquette

ISBN 0-373-83272-9

ANNIVERSARY WALTZ

One

She wasn't married?

The piece of paper in her trembling hand had to be wrong! Megan *knew* she was married!

She stared at the document. ''This license must be filed with City Hall for marriage of above couple to become effective,'' it stated.

Her license, her *marriage* license, hadn't been filed! She was holding the original in her hand! Could it possibly be true? She, Mrs. Reed Kendall, was still Miss Megan McCullough?

She read the bold red-print warning again. Why hadn't the license been filed? Wasn't that the best man's job?

''Dear Lord, no...'' Megan moaned.

Jerry Davis, her dearest friend in the world, had been best man at the wedding. But Jerry was not a real best man. He hadn't wanted Megan to marry Reed. He'd wanted Megan to marry *him.*

''I'm telling you, Meggie, this guy isn't for you. It's not too late to change your mind,'' Jerry had pleaded the night before the wedding. They were at the church for the rehearsal; the two of them had been early and were waiting for everyone else to arrive.

"Jerry, I'm nervous enough as it is!" Megan scowled furiously at him. "And don't use my nickname. You know Reed hates it."

Jerry scowled back. "Your parents and friends have called you Meggie since you were an infant. So what if Reed doesn't approve? This is exactly what I'm talking about. The man has you under his thumb already, and the ring's not even on your finger. I'm warning you, it's only going to get worse!"

"Shh!" Megan looked around to see if anyone had heard, but they were still alone. She wished she was already married. By this time tomorrow she would be, and then—

"What's the matter? Afraid your darling Reed might not approve of your talking to me?"

"It's not that—"

"Of course it is." Jerry paced the floor of the church entryway. "I still can't believe he allowed me to be in the wedding party."

"He's an only child. He doesn't have any brothers."

"He has friends, though, and I'm not one of them. You must have brought out the heavy-duty artillery to even get me an invitation, let alone serve as his best man."

"Reed knows that you and I grew up together. He understands how close we are. He was more than happy to include you," Megan said, wincing at the lie. She *hated* lies.

Jerry gave a hollow laugh. "Oh, he understands, all right. He knows I think you're making the biggest mistake of your life. Which you are."

"Jerry, please!" Megan was nearly in tears. "Tomorrow is my wedding day!"

Jerry's jaw set in an ugly line. "Don't you think I know that? I know you'll never marry me. I know you love me like a brother. That part's bad enough. But if I can't make you happy, I at least want you to marry someone who will!"

Megan reached for Jerry's hands. "Reed will."

Jerry shook his head. "He won't. Reed doesn't know the meaning of the word 'compromise.' By this time next year, you'll be miserable. He's an arrogant, conceited, selfish son of a—"

"Jerry! We're in a church!"

Jerry sighed. "He's the kind of man who sets women's rights back fifty years. First he'll make you give up your friends, starting with me. Then he'll make you give up your job. Then it will be your family, and who *knows* what's next. Meggie, don't you see? The man doesn't share. What's his is his, and you're about to become another possession. You can't live that kind of life. You'll wither and die! I know you!"

"You're wrong." Megan looked straight into the eyes of her friend. "And even if you weren't, I'd marry him anyway. I love him, Jerry. I love him so much it hurts."

Jerry exhaled slowly and heavily. "Don't I know it." He closed his eyes, then opened them again. "Well, you're a big girl now. But mark my words. You won't make it to your first anniversary without battle scars. One year and you'll be begging for a divorce."

Megan pushed aside her friend's dire warning. "Reed and I love each other. Everything will be fine. You wait and see." But her words sounded forced, even to her. Oh, where *was* everyone?

"You and Reed—you're both too different! Twelve months, Meggie. That's all I give you."

The two old friends had stared at one another in silence until suddenly there was a commotion just outside the door, and they'd both turned to see her future husband walk in. His eyes narrowed as he noted how close Jerry was standing to Megan.

"If you ever need me, I'm here for you," Jerry had whispered to her. "You call, and I'll come running."

She'd nodded and squeezed his hand, hating the pain she was causing him. Then she turned away from her lifelong companion and friend. She even managed a smile as Reed, his manner proprietary, even haughty, tucked his arm in hers. Then Megan McCullough turned her back on Jerry's warnings, got through the rehearsal, survived her sleepless night, and the next day became Mrs. Reed Kendall.

That was more than ten months ago. Megan moaned as she remembered her wedding day. She put down the unfiled marriage license and buried her face in her hands. As the tears fell, she realized that everything Jerry had prophesied had come true. . . .

First her friends, then her job, then her family had fallen away, all casualties of her love for Reed. They hadn't been deliberate requests on Reed's part or conscious actions on Megan's, but somehow she had ended up with no one in her life but him. And she was still in love with Reed—knew she'd always love him—but how much more would she lose proving it?

Damn Jerry for being right! No, damn Reed for always having the upper hand. Reed might be happy, but Megan wasn't. The dreary existence she now led was slowly draining her. She wanted her life back.

Megan picked up the couriered envelope in which the license had been delivered. Looking inside, she saw a key and two sheets of paper with writing on them. She picked up the first one.

"Dear Meggie," it read, "surprise, surprise! I know it's a shock, but as you can see, I never filed your marriage license. This is kind of hard to explain, but here goes."

Agitated, Megan pushed back a long strand of hair and kept reading.

"I got pretty drunk at the wedding reception, remember?"

Oh, yes, he certainly had. Megan also remembered that Reed's dark disapproval had taken some of the joy out of the day.

"Every time I saw Reed I had another drink," Jerry continued. "I ended up not filing the license out of sheer spite. After I sobered up, I decided to call my lawyer. According to him, you have one year to file a marriage license before it becomes invalid. In addition, until it is filed, you're not legally married."

Good Lord, she wasn't married, after all!

"I know it was a crazy thing to do, but I decided to save you from a fate worse than death—marriage to Reed Kendall. After seeing how miserable he's made you, I'm glad I did."

The word "glad" was underlined three times.

"Reed will never give you a divorce, Megan. We both know that. So I'm sending you your ticket to freedom. Burn this license, and you're home free. Keep it, file it with City Hall, and you'll end up an unhappy, bitter woman—if you aren't already."

She wasn't bitter, she told herself. She wasn't. But she *was* unhappy, desperately so.

"Your anniversary is in six weeks. You have that long to decide. It's your choice. I love you. Jerry."

Megan put the letter down and unfolded the other sheet of paper with trembling hands. "I just had an idea, Meggie. I've decided to leave you the key to my safe-deposit box. If I know my cautious Meggie, you won't burn the license right away. So lock it away for safekeeping until you decide for certain. I'm upstate on business, but will call you tonight."

Megan breathed a sigh of relief on learning that Jerry was out of harm's way. She might have the fiery Irish ancestors, but Reed's temper was the volatile one. She feared for Jerry's safety when Reed found out.

When? She meant *if*. Megan shook her head. Was she actually contemplating telling Reed?

She picked up the license and looked from it to the second note and back again, feeling more than a touch of hysteria. Finally she dropped them both, along with the safe-deposit key, into her bag. Her heart was racing.

To start over again! The idea was so tempting. Maybe *too* tempting! Her marriage must really be on shaky ground for her even to consider going through with Jerry's suggestion. Reed loved her, and she loved him. No matter what their problems, that was never in doubt. Suddenly Megan needed the reassurance of her husband's voice.

She dialed his private office number but reached his secretary, instead.

"Good afternoon. Kendall Diamond Brokerage. Barbara speaking."

"This is..." Megan Kendall? Megan McCullough? Who was she? "Megan," she finally said. "May I speak to Reed, please?"

"Oh, good afternoon, Mrs. Kendall. Your husband's not in the office right now."

Megan's face fell with disappointment. "Can you tell me when he will be?"

"He just left for the airport. He's flying out of town to meet a customer about some African gem purchases. He won't be back until tomorrow." There was an awkward pause. "Didn't he tell you?"

"No. No, he didn't."

"Would you like me to have him call you? I can still reach him in the limo, if you wish."

"I..." Megan struggled for control, hating the sound of pity in the older woman's voice. This wasn't the first time Megan had been embarrassed by Reed's lack of thoughtfulness. "Never mind. I'll talk to him later. Goodbye."

She replaced the receiver with uncharacteristic viciousness, then picked up the unfiled marriage license. She had to get away from this house—the house where she'd spent so many lonely nights waiting for Reed to come home. She had to think!

Suddenly she knew what she had to do. She grabbed her bag, checked the name and address of the bank, which Jerry had written on the key's paper tag, then hurried outside to her car. Jerry said she had six weeks to make up her mind. She was going to use the time, rethink her life. In the meantime, she'd lock the license safely away from Reed.

Megan's hands were shaking so badly it took her three tries to get the car key into the ignition.

They were still shaking when she reached the bank. Even the bank clerk noticed.

"Are you all right, ma'am?" he asked. "Can I get you a glass of water or something?"

"No, no, nothing. I just want to get to Jerry's—to my safe-deposit box."

"I didn't know Mr. Davis had a wife," the clerk said. "I hope he's as good a husband as he is a customer here."

"He's not my husband!" Megan's voice was so loud a few customers glanced her way. How could they know that, as of today, she didn't even *have* a husband?

The clerk apologized profusely, but Megan was too upset to wonder what conclusions he was drawing about her and Jerry's relationship.

"Please follow me. I'll explain the procedure to you, since you haven't been here before. You see, the box can only be opened with a bank key and your key." He led Megan into the vault. "If you were to lose yours, we'd have to conduct an investigation before we could issue you another. That could take months, so guard it carefully."

Megan thought of Reed and nodded vigorously.

"Here we are. Hand me your key, and I'll open your box."

He did so, leaving Megan to gaze into the empty drawer. Why was she here? She must be crazy! She should be downtown at City Hall in the clerk's office, filing her marriage certificate.

Megan thought of being in bed with Reed. How her heart filled with joy every time he brought her body to that sweet fever pitch! How he loved to kiss her and hold her and talk with her—on the rare occasions he was home. She'd fallen in love with Reed the first time she'd laid eyes on him. She loved him still—his face, his laugh, the way he stretched and immediately reached for her when he awoke in the morning.

Could she really give that up without tearing her heart in two?

"Ma'am? I'll leave if you want privacy."

Megan thought of all the lonely nights when Reed was away. She remembered his broken promises to spend more time with her if she'd quit her job.

"Our schedules are just too busy, Megan," he had gently chided. "And you know I can't work around *my* hours."

She remembered all the phone calls from friends begging her to get back into circulation. She remembered not wanting to go without Reed, who was always working. And so she never went at all until little by little the invitations stopped.

Megan hardened her heart. "You can wait here," she told the clerk. "This will only take a second." She reached into her purse and removed the license. With just the slightest hesitation, she put it into the cold steel box and locked it away.

"I'm done."

As Megan walked toward the exit, she heard the clerk say, "Remember, take care of that key."

"I will." She had to. Her happiness—and Reed's—depended on it.

Once outside, Megan tore off the key's identifying paper tag and threw it into the bank's garbage can. Back in the car, she put the bank key on her key chain. There was no way Reed could go after the license now. And once—*if*—he found out, he *would* go after it. Megan was absolutely certain.

Whatever his faults, Reed loved her with a strength that was almost frightening. He believed in loyalty until "death do us part." He would never let her go, especially with Jerry waiting in the wings. The fact that Jerry had never married had always been a sore spot with Reed.

Well, she just wouldn't tell him, Megan decided. She had six weeks to decide—six weeks to see if she and Reed could work out their problems. In the meantime, she might as well go home and wait for Jerry's call. Jerry had wreaked enough havoc in her life for one day. She had to make certain he'd leave well enough—that being Reed—alone. Her nerves were already stretched to the breaking point; she didn't want to deal with Reed's temper, too.

As usual, Los Angeles rush-hour traffic was a mess, and Megan found herself moving nowhere. The events of the day suddenly overwhelmed her, and she rested her forehead against the steering wheel.

"What have I done? Oh, Reed, what's happened to us?" she whispered.

The ringing of the car phone startled her. Megan never got calls. She remembered when Reed first bought her the expensive sports car and loaded it with every possible option. They'd still been newlyweds, and Reed still the smitten groom.

"Reed, you shouldn't spend so much money on me. I'll never use a car phone," she had said, laughing.

"I can afford it. You deserve the best." He'd grinned. "Besides, what better way for us to keep in touch?"

But he'd always been too busy to keep in touch with anyone who wasn't business-related. Wives, it seemed, were low on the totem pole. Or rather, she corrected herself wryly, the telephone pole.

The phone rang again just as Megan lifted her head and reached for the receiver. Maybe it was Jerry calling, telling her this was all a bad joke.

"Hello, Mrs. Kendall? This is Barbara, again, and I have a message from your husband."

Megan fought her embarrassment. "Yes, Barbara?"

"I called Mr. Kendall after you and I talked. He was quite upset at forgetting to inform you of his plans. He said to tell you he's canceled his flight."

"Canceled?"

"That's right. He'll be home for dinner, after all."

Megan felt cold fear course through her veins. The first page of Jerry's letter was still on the coffee table! And she was miles from home and stuck in traffic.

"Tell him I'm not at home! Tell him to wait for me at the office," she said frantically.

"I'm sorry, Mrs. Kendall," Barbara murmured. "Mr. Kendall left the airport an hour ago."

Megan's breath caught in her throat.

"He should be home already."

Two

Megan sat in shock, oblivious to the traffic now inching forward. Several angry horns blew at her from behind. With a start, she hung up the phone and took her foot off the brake. Another horn blared at her slow response, and suddenly Megan was remembering. A blaring horn was how she and Reed had met....

It was two years ago. She'd stepped off a bush plane in the middle of nowhere with one small suitcase in hand and a new ID card in her pants pocket. Her name, Megan McCullough, was emblazoned under the Kendall Diamond Mines logo.

The air was hot and humid, the plane smelled of gasoline and other unpleasant cargo, and a dismayed Megan saw no one waiting to greet her.

"End of the line," the pilot yelled. "Someone will meet you sooner or later."

"But—"

"Your ticket was one way, luv. Get off the strip!"

Megan did. She watched with apprehension as the plane took off, leaving her alone, somewhere in Africa's diamond country.

She had ten minutes by herself, just enough time to wonder what she was doing there. Why in the world had she left her safe job back home to work in a foreign clinic? How could she have left Jerry behind? Had she finally bitten off more than she could chew?

Then a horn sounded, and one look at the man in the Jeep chased away all those fears. The first thing Megan noticed was his vitality. He hit the horn again, waved his arm and gave her a welcoming smile that made her feel all was right with the world. She exhaled a sigh of relief, and waited for his approach.

The breeze blew glossy strands of black hair over the driver's tanned forehead. And as the Jeep came even closer and pulled to a stop, Megan saw the intelligence in his eyes.

"Need a lift, stranger?" he asked in a deep voice.

His partially buttoned khaki shirt revealed a muscled chest and broad shoulders, but there was no masculine preening evident in his person. Megan instinctively knew that this was a man supremely confident with who and what he was.

"If you're from Kendall, I do."

"And if I'm not?"

Megan glanced around at the jungle desolation. "I'll take my chances." She threw her suitcase into the back of the Jeep and climbed in, missing his look of admiration.

"Aren't you going to ask for my identification?" he asked.

Megan shook her head and fastened her seat belt. "It wouldn't make any difference if you were a saint or an ax murderer. My plane is gone and I'm alone in a jungle—for the very first time, I might add—so either way I'm at your mercy. Whoever you are, I'm pleased to meet you. Meggie McCullough."

She held out her hand for him to shake, and this time she did see the admiration in his gaze as he took in her green eyes and lustrous red-gold hair. He took her hand, but instead of shaking it, gently held it.

"Reed Kendall, at your service."

Megan blinked in surprise, then frowned. "Look, I've had a long flight, and I'm in no mood for practical jokes. I'm sure Mr. Kendall has better things to do with his time than play chauffeur."

His eyes were merry. "I probably do, but I decided to take the day off. I needed a reason to get away, and you, Miss McCullough, provided a delightful one." His brown eyes twinkled as he released her hand to shift the Jeep into gear.

Megan found herself blushing at the compliment.

"Still worried I'm an ax murderer?" Reed asked as the vehicle picked up speed and he shifted again into higher gear.

Megan refused to be baited. "Or an imposter. Either way, you're quite charming for a criminal."

Reed gave a totally masculine grin. He reached into the breast pocket of his safari shirt. "Here, read this. Such bravery deserves a reward."

Megan took the plastic-laminated photo ID from his hand, and read it aloud. "Reed Kendall. Kendall Diamond Mines."

She knew he was waiting for a response, but she refused to act the cowering employee. She gazed at the photo and then back at him. "I'm pleased to meet you, Mr. Kendall. But why are *you* here?"

Reed took his eyes off the road to give her a quick glance. "As opposed to another member of my staff?"

"Yes. You must admit it's strange to have the big boss himself pick up new employees at the airstrip."

"Not if he wants to meet each new employee and evaluate him—or her—in person." Megan must have looked unconvinced, because he added, "If I were just out to impress people, I'd put my logo and title on the Jeep."

He wouldn't even need to do that, Megan thought to herself. Reed Kendall was a handsome man, but there was something more than just his looks that appealed to her. She was trying to get a handle on exactly what that was when he said, "We have a long drive ahead of us. Tell me about yourself, Megan McCullough."

"Well, I prefer Meggie to Megan, for starters. I graduated from college in Philadelphia. I have a degree in nursing, and—"

"I want more than just what's on your job application," he interrupted. Suddenly the cheerful voice of the stranger was replaced with the authoritative command of a supervisor. "I've read that."

"Then what would you like to know?"

"Start with your family. How many, how close are you all, and why did they let you come to Africa?"

As Megan tied back her hair to keep it from whipping across her face, she related her family history. "Well, I'm the oldest of six children, and one of four girls. My parents are both first-generation Americans. The family's originally from Ireland. Dad's worked the Pennsylvania steel mills all his life, and Mom's stayed home and raised the family. My parents have been happily married for more than thirty years."

"A rarity," Reed said with a strange expression.

"Thirty years?"

"That, and the happy part. My parents aren't, although they pretend quite well. Go on, Megan."

Megan would much rather have questioned him about *his* parents, but he was her employer. He had the right to call her by her legal first name, instead of her nickname, and ask personal questions. She didn't.

"You asked why they let me come to Africa," she said slowly. "It wasn't a question of getting their permission. I'm twenty-seven years old, hardly a child. I love my family, of course, but I never intended to spend my whole life in my hometown. Since graduation, I've worked in the hospital there, but I decided it was time for a change, and here I am."

"Hmm." Reed didn't sound quite satisfied with her answer. "Most women nowadays want to be lawyers or stockbrokers or high-powered executives. The nursing profession seems almost old-fashioned in these times. I should know. We hardly had anyone respond to our advertisement for a clinic nurse. Why nursing, Megan? How did I end up with you?"

"I..." Megan hesitated, then decided to tell the truth. "I grew up in a hospital."

Reed gave her a sharp look, then turned back toward the road. "You spent a lot of time there?"

"No, I mean I grew up there. I entered one when I was nine and was discharged when I was seventeen. I ate, drank, slept, played and went to school there."

There was silence. Then, "I'm surprised you could even bear to be around the medical profession after an experience like that."

Megan sat up straight with surprise. She'd expected the usual sympathy and the lame platitudes she'd heard a hundred times before. Instead, she was awed by his insight.

"I couldn't, not at first. I hated hospitals, doctors and nurses with a passion. I despised being there and was angry with my parents for abandoning me."

"What changed your mind?"

She thought about that. "More than anything, I wanted to be normal."

"What was wrong with you?"

Megan appreciated Reed's bluntness. "I was born with congenital birth defects of my right hip and leg. Oh, I'm all right now," she said at his concerned look. "My passing your company's medical exam is proof of that. But as a child, I was never able to walk. My brothers and sisters would run and play, and I—" Megan smiled at the memory "—I sat in a wheelchair and cried. I was quite pathetic, really."

"That's understandable, considering," Reed said compassionately. "What happened?"

"Dad's medical insurance wouldn't cover all the treatment I needed, or all the time I'd be in the hospital. Mom sent in an application to Shriners Hospital for Children. They pay for everything if you're admitted."

"You were one of the lucky ones?"

"Yes. Mom packed me a suitcase and I left home." Megan shook her head. "I had no idea it would be for so long."

"But you were cured. Surely it was worth it."

"There was a price, though. When I left home, I lost my family. I grew up alone. My brothers and sisters grew up without me. Oh, I saw them during visiting hours from time to time, but it wasn't the same. Dad was working, and Mom was busy with the other children." Megan's eyes were sad. "When I was finally released, they were strangers to me—and I to them. I suppose in a way they still are."

Reed was silent. The only sound was the Jeep's engine.

After a moment she continued, "The nurses and the other children in my situation became my surrogate family. There were a few special ones, especially among the patients."

Like Jerry Davis. He had been another patient with orthopedic birth defects. The two of them were admitted to the hospital on the same day. As they were the same age, they went to school together. Jerry became the surrogate brother, the surrogate kin, replacing the family Megan had lost. They shared the same doctors, therapists and teachers; they also shared childish confidences and very real physical pain. They even shared a love for medicine. Jerry had gone on to medical school when Megan entered nursing.

"And they inspired you to join the profession?"

Megan nodded, inexplicably comfortable confiding in this stranger. "Who better to take care of patients than someone like me? I understand their needs more than anyone."

"I imagine you do. But why here, Megan? Why a clinic at a diamond mine in Africa? We don't have the kind of patients—or injuries—you've probably worked with."

Megan remembered her initial interview at the employment agency. She'd be caring for those injured while blasting and mining for diamonds—the casualties of a risky profession.

She also remembered Jerry Davis begging her not to leave, reminding her of all the years they were patients at the hospital together. And knowing she could never love him the way he wanted.

"We're so much alike, Meggie," he'd said. "We've shared so much already. Don't go, sweetheart. Stay here and marry me."

But she couldn't, and that was why she was in Africa. Megan had requested an extended leave of absence at the hospital where she'd first been admitted and then employed, the same place Jerry had come back to work as a surgeon specializing in pediatrics. She'd wanted a temporary job that would take her far away.

She couldn't stand to keep refusing him. Like Megan, Jerry had suffered enough hurt in his life. She could only pray that during her absence his emotional wounds would heal.

She turned toward Reed Kendall and gave him a noncommittal answer. "I needed a change of scenery."

"As good a reason as any."

Megan was relieved when the personal questions stopped. She couldn't know that the pain in her eyes was visible for him to see. She only knew that it was far easier to listen to Reed talk about her new job.

"Mining is hard on the machinery and even harder on the human body. I've implemented the most up-to-date safety procedures available, but accidents do occur. That's where you come in. You'll be at the aid station right at the mine."

"I won't be at your clinic?"

"The clinic is away from the mine and all the adjacent blast sites. I need someone on the scene who can handle the day-to-day cuts and scrapes we get. More importantly, I want any serious injuries triaged and treated. I don't want anyone dying en route to the clinic if I can help it."

Megan stared at him with amazement and a growing respect. Diamond mining was an expensive, speculative business. Yet Reed seemed to spare no expense when it came to protecting his employees.

She was later to discover that the man was full of surprises. The initial attraction she felt for him increased into something deeper as the weeks, then months, passed. And wonder of wonders, her feelings were returned. She and Reed gradually spent more and more time with each other, until even the employees knew that something special was happening.

She remembered, oh, so clearly, the night they had first made love. She'd been at his bungalow, watching him strip off a grimy, sweat-stained shirt in front of the kitchen sink. "You really graduated from Harvard?" Megan was asking.

"Summa cum laude, with a master's degree in business and finance. Courtesy of my parents and old money."

He turned on the taps full bore and sluiced his hands and face with water and soap. Megan watched the play of muscles across his back and waited until he was finished.

"Surely you don't need to work so hard for a living, then, Reed. Why did you give up easy street for this?" she asked as he dried himself.

Reed came over and kissed her nose. "Because, my sweet, I had no wish to live my life as the only son and heir of Mr. and Mrs. Kendall." He sank into the kitchen chair opposite her and gave his wet hair a careless swipe with the towel. "My mother never wanted children, but my father held the purse strings. No son, no pocket money, he told Mother, and so I was reluctantly conceived."

"Reed, that sounds so..." Megan's voice trailed off uncertainly.

"Cold-blooded? It was. But Mother considers herself lucky. I wasn't a daughter, so she only had to go through the ordeal—her words, not mine—of being pregnant once. Father had his heir—someone who would take over the Kendall tradition of dabbling in assorted stocks and equally assorted women."

Megan watched in dismay as Reed tossed the towel over the sink, then picked up the drink Megan had fixed for him.

"You needn't look so shocked. It's all quite civilized. Mother is allowed her playmates, too. However, I decided that wasn't for me. I didn't want to be a playboy living off Father's money."

Megan couldn't believe the turn the conversation had taken, for Reed had never talked about his family. She was afraid any comments from her might put a sudden end to it, so she remained silent.

"Unknown to my parents, I worked all through college. Did you know construction pays remarkably well?" Reed lifted an eyebrow as Megan shook her head. "Well, it does. And because of that, I was able to play the stock market. But I didn't do it for fun, like Father had taught me. I played for keeps. After graduation, I took what money I'd earned and made more." He gave her an understated look of triumph. "And more."

"Your parents must have been proud of you," Megan ventured.

"Hardly," Reed drawled. "Father hated me because he couldn't hold his money over my head and make me jump through hoops. And Mother hated me for the same reason. Misery does love company, you know."

Megan didn't like the expression in Reed's eyes. It was more than unpleasant, it was downright frightening. Reed pushed away his drink, his gaze unfocused as he remembered the past.

"So, I paid Father back for my fancy expensive education. With interest, of course. Then I left home for good to try my hand at something new."

He looked back at Megan, and tenderness replaced the dreadful bleakness in his eyes.

"I like taking risks, but I also like excitement. The stock market was useful, but it wasn't what I wanted as a career. One thing led to another, and here I am, grateful for the best thing that's ever come my way."

"The diamond mine?" Megan ventured.

"No." Reed rose from his chair and gently pulled her into his arms. "You."

It was as if a long-standing barrier had fallen. Reed opened himself up to her both physically and emotionally. There was no more holding back.

And when Reed gathered her close and made them as one, Megan felt herself reborn in the beauty of their joining. The years of loneliness in the hospital fell away. The years of having no real family of her own disappeared, and there was only Megan, and Reed, and their love for each other.

The feeling remained in the days that followed. Megan found herself swept into the life of a man who now was everything to her.

"I love you, Megan McCullough," Reed said to her for the very first time one night. He didn't whisper it into her ear or accompany his declaration with sweet murmurs. He spoke the words clearly, so that she could hear every syllable. "I've waited all my life for a woman like you."

A feeling of joy spread through her, rendering her momentarily speechless. She nestled against his bare chest as he held her even tighter.

"I love you, too, Reed." She kissed him, feeling at home and content in his arms. That contentment was replaced by pure happiness at his next words.

"Be my wife, Megan. Marry me."

Megan sat up in his arms, eyes shining. Her reply was on her lips, but Reed laid a finger across them, silencing her.

"Wait. Before you give me your answer, there's something I want you to know. As your husband, I'll do everything within my power to make you happy. But in return, I want you to be faithful to me. Utterly loyal. No lies. I won't marry you without that promise, Megan."

His eyes were dark with emotion. Megan remembered what he'd said about his parents, and the mockery they'd made of their marriage. It was a wonder their son still believed in the institution.

"I promise, Reed."

He wasn't satisfied. "I mean for life, Megan," he warned. "Until death do us part. If that's too much to ask, then I'm not the man for you."

"You *are*, Reed. Pledging myself to you is no sacrifice. It's what I want." And she sealed her promise with a kiss.

His arms tightened around her and his lips seared hers with a passion that soon had her trembling with urgent need. Their lovemaking that night was different for both of them. Reed revealed a power and intensity he'd formerly restrained. Megan couldn't help recognizing the difference any more than she could prevent what had happened.

And from then on, she was his....

Three

Megan pulled into the private road that led to their beachfront home. Usually the rolling green breakers of the Pacific soothed her spirits, but she was in no state to enjoy the summer sunset this evening.

Where had all the joy between her and Reed gone? They had left Africa to settle near Reed's California offices with newly wedded bliss and high hopes. Those had quickly disappeared as Reed became more and more caught up in his business.

If it hadn't been for Jerry Davis's sudden decision to leave Pennsylvania and practice medicine in Los Angeles, Megan would have been lost. Both she and Reed knew the move was prompted by Jerry's feelings for Megan. Megan herself had advised Jerry against it, but Jerry had been firm.

"With Reed for a husband, you'll need a friend, Meggie."

Megan frowned at the memory. Some friend Jerry had turned out to be. Look at the mess she was in now.

She saw Reed's car in the driveway and steeled herself for the task ahead.

Megan walked inside. The cheery "Reed, I'm home" she'd planned died on her lips. Reed was standing in front of the fireplace. His expensive jacket and tie were tossed on the hardwood floor with uncharacteristic abandon.

"No wonder Barbara thought you were upset." Reed held up Jerry's letter, then crumpled it viciously, tossing it with a savage motion to the floor. "It seems you've had quite a day."

Megan placed her purse on the coffee table. "That, Reed, has to be the understatement of the year." She sank onto the couch and closed her eyes, trying to collect her thoughts.

After a moment, she felt his weight beside her, then felt his fingers tenderly stroking her hair. "This fiasco doesn't make us any less married, Megan." He placed a gentle kiss on her hair. "We'll file the damn thing first thing tomorrow, if you haven't already, and that will be the end of it."

Megan opened her eyes. "Will it, Reed?" Her voice sounded like that of a stranger, and Reed froze.

"What's that supposed to mean?" he asked.

She shook her head and didn't answer.

"Megan?" Reed's voice was harsh with urgency. "Answer me!"

"I didn't file the license," she finally said.

"But you're going to, right?"

Megan looked away. Reed's hands flew to her shoulders.

"Where's the license?" he asked hoarsely. "Megan, look at me!"

She did, her eyes full of pain.

"Tell me what you did with the license."

She felt sick inside, not wanting to hurt him but knowing he deserved an answer. "I locked it up."

"You . . ." He couldn't finish.

Her next words came out so softly he had to strain to hear them. "I don't know if I want to be married to you anymore."

There was silence in the room. Then Reed angrily rose to his feet. He walked to the huge bay window overlooking the beach and took a deep breath. Megan watched him carefully. She wasn't fooled into thinking he would remain calm. His clenched fists and next words confirmed it.

"Damn Jerry Davis to hell! If he were here now, I'd wring his neck!"

"Jerry has nothing to do with this!"

Reed whirled around at that. "I see. Our wedding license should have filed itself," he said sarcastically. "Wake up, Megan. The man is still in love with you! This latest stunt proves it. He's never accepted our marriage. He never will."

"He's never accepted the fact that I'm unhappy."

Reed's angry tirade stopped abruptly. "You're unhappy?" he repeated in a shocked voice. "I make you unhappy, Megan?"

"Yes." The single syllable escaped her lips before she could prevent it. At Reed's stricken expression, she held out her hand to him. "Reed, come sit down. Let me try to explain."

He did, and Megan studied him with love in her heart. His eyes were dark with confusion and hurt. The self-assured air that was so much a part of him was badly shaken. They held too much power over each other, she suddenly realized.

She must have spoken aloud, for Reed echoed her words.

"Too much power? Megan, I don't understand. We love each other! The one thing I've always been sure of is that."

"Sometimes we love each other too much, Reed." Megan reached for his hands. "You take me for granted, and I let you. We're both at fault."

Reed gently traced her palms with his thumbs. "This is about today, isn't it? Because I forgot to tell you I was going out of town. Megan, I'm sorry."

"It's more than just that!" Megan snatched her hands away in irritation. "I have no life of my own anymore. I have no job, no friends, and I never get back to see my family. I've put my life on hold to try and spend more time with you, but it hasn't worked. You're never here, and I'm miserable."

"I'll try to clear up my schedule some, and—"

"I've heard that story before!" Megan said sharply, getting to her feet. "I'm tired of waiting. I'm tired of your promises. You're a wealthy man, yet you'd rather spend all your time making more money, instead of spending time with your wife. I'm tired of that, too!"

Reed stood with her, capturing her arm when she would have strode away. "My God, Megan, is that how you see things?"

"What am I supposed to think?" she asked bitterly. "You're *never* here. And I'm not a part of your life anymore, like I was in Africa. I'm just a convenience. And sometimes, it feels like I'm not even that." To her horror, tears started falling from her eyes. She, who never cried in front of others, not even during all those years in the hospital.

"Megan, don't," Reed said, holding her face in his hands. "I'll do better by you, I swear." He kissed the corner of her eye, then her cheek, then started a butter-fly-light trail down her neck.

"I love you, Megan. You know I do."

She nodded. That was all the signal Reed needed. His mouth came down hard on hers and he pulled her to him. In his arms she was his willing prisoner. Under his touch she came alive as she never did with anyone else.

Then they were in bed, their clothes on the floor, their bodies close.

"Reed, why can't it be like this all the time?" Megan whispered as his hands set her pulses racing with de-sire. It had been weeks since they'd made love, because Reed had been staying late at the office. "Is your work so important?"

"It's nothing compared to you, my love. Nothing." Then his mouth covered hers, and his body covered hers, and there was no more talking. There was only Reed and Megan, and the magic they had together.

"I must be the world's biggest idiot," Reed said later. They lay entwined in each other's arms, spent with passion. "Sending you to bed alone night after night."

Megan propped her head on her hand and studied him. "Then why do you, Reed?"

He shrugged. "I get so caught up in my work. Be-lieve it or not, Megan, I enjoy what I do. I could never be like my father. He had money in the bank, so his conscience was clear when he let life pass him by."

But life was passing her by, too, Megan thought. Her honesty compelled her to say, "That's me, Reed. I'm just like him."

He smiled, unwilling to take her seriously. "Don't be silly, Megan. You're not at all like him." He gave her one last kiss on the nose. "Now go to sleep. I want you at the city clerk's office first thing tomorrow morning.''

But Megan couldn't sleep. Long after Reed had dropped off, she lay awake, her mind in turmoil. Reed was very generous. He considered everything that was his, hers, and Megan had more money than she knew what to do with. Then, suddenly, she felt ashamed, for Reed's wealth had allowed her to sit home and do nothing.

But Reed wasn't the only guilty party to her unhappiness. She had caused much of it herself.

Reed stirred in his sleep, and Megan studied him with hope in her heart. At least they were finally being honest with each other. Perhaps now things would get better between them.

She made up her mind. She would file her marriage license tomorrow morning, just as Reed suggested. In fact, they could both do it. It had been ages since they'd spent a day together. Maybe they could look in on some of the friends they'd neglected for so long.

Megan sighed with contentment. She placed one arm around Reed's sleeping form and was just about to close her eyes when the phone rang.

She grabbed the phone on the bedside stand before it could ring a second time.

"Hi, Meggie. It's me."

"Jerry!" Megan turned in alarm toward Reed, but he slept on.

"At your service. So, enjoy your day?"

"No, I didn't, thanks to you," she hissed. "I thought you were my friend, Jerry! I trusted you! I didn't appreciate your little surprise, and neither did Reed."

"You actually went and told him?" Jerry gave a slow whistle. "Meggie, you're braver than I thought."

"It was an accident. I left your letter on the coffee table when I went to the bank. Reed found it when he came home."

"So you didn't go to City Hall, after all," Jerry said with real pleasure. "I didn't think you would. And Reed actually came home for a change. I wish I could have seen his face when he heard the news."

"No, you don't, Jerry. He said he wanted to break your neck!" Reed stirred at her vehemence. Megan watched anxiously as he settled down again, then lowered her voice. "And if you were here, I might have let him. You had no right to interfere in my marriage."

Jerry laughed sarcastically. "What marriage, Miss McCullough?"

"Jerry, I'm warning you..."

"All right, I'll behave." Jerry suddenly grew serious again. "Meggie, I just want you to be happy. If it's Reed you really want, then make him appreciate you! Use that license as a weapon. I guarantee you it's a powerful one."

"I don't play those kinds of games with Reed, and you know it."

"And that's why he's walked all over you. I love you dearly, Meggie mine, but that doormat complex of yours has got to go. Or else your marriage will pay the price."

Megan cringed at his words. "We did talk, Jerry. Everything's okay now."

"Oh, Meggie...you are so naive. You and Reed have a real problem. I'd bet my last cent all you got from him was a kiss and a promise, and an empty one at that. You can't just expect everything to be better in the morning. If I know Reed, he isn't going to change overnight."

Megan felt a vague sense of unease. They hadn't talked much, it was true. Reed had been hurt, she'd been upset, then somehow they'd ended up in bed together. Just as Jerry had guessed.

"Don't do anything rash, Meggie. Guard that license with your life. If Reed wants you, let him fight for you! Don't make things easy for him anymore."

"He said he'd try harder, Jerry," Megan insisted. "He really did."

"You're a fool, Megan McCullough. A damned fool!"

"If I am, that's my business. Mine and Reed's. Not yours."

There was silence on the other end of the line. Then, "I suppose I deserved that. I'll stand aside—for now. But I'm warning you, Meggie, nothing's going to change. And if Reed doesn't want you anymore, then I do."

Jerry hung up. Megan replaced the receiver with trembling fingers. If it wasn't so tragic, it would be almost funny. The man she wanted most in the world was rarely there for her, while the man she could never love always was.

Megan lay down again and forced herself to close her eyes. Jerry was wrong. Everything between her and Reed would be fine.

Sometime during the night Megan finally fell asleep. When she awoke, Reed was in front of the dresser mirror, knotting his tie.

"Reed?"

"Good morning, sweetheart."

Megan raised her head to check the alarm clock. "It's only five-thirty. Where are you going?"

"To work, of course." He finished with the tie. "But I'll be home early, I promise." He reached for his jacket on the back of the chair.

Megan sat up, clutching the sheet to her chest. "But...I thought we could spend the day together. It's been ages since you took any time off."

"I took time off yesterday, Megan. That's why I have to go in today. I'm running behind." He slid his wallet into his pocket. "I'll try to call you at lunch. Don't forget to file the license with the city clerk."

He gave her a quick kiss on the cheek, then picked up his car keys. "I'm going to be late. Have a good day now."

"But, Reed!"

"I'll try to call you."

"When?"

There was no answer. He was already gone. Megan was alone again, with nothing to look forward to except a phone call that might or might not come. Suddenly she saw herself years from now, still alone, still waiting for the phone to ring.

An icy chill ran through her veins. Megan felt more than just alone. She felt lifeless.

Something had to change. She stood up with determination and headed for the shower. Her linen skirt and silk blouse would be just the thing for job-hunting. She'd be at the door of the employment office at her old L.A. workplace the minute they opened.

They were always looking for good nurses, she knew. She wasn't coming home until she'd received a bona fide offer of employment. And then...

Megan turned on the shower and reached for the shampoo. Then she was going to hunt up her old address book and call or write every single one of her friends and family. It might take a few weeks, even longer, to rekindle her personal life, but her mind was made up.

Mrs. Kendall was gone. Reed or no Reed, Meggie McCullough was back.

Four

"Where the hell have you been?" Reed said the minute Megan walked in the house. "It's almost midnight!"

Megan looked at her watch. Goodness, but it *was* late! For the first time in months, she'd actually had a day where time didn't hang heavily on her hands. She smiled with real satisfaction.

"I'm glad you find this amusing." Reed took her jacket and purse from her, his movements revealing a barely controlled anger. "I've been worried sick!"

But Reed's ill temper couldn't spoil Megan's mood. "Why? You've come home much later than this, and I'm not allowed to complain."

Reed slammed her purse down on the mantel with a roughness that didn't bode well for its contents. "Have you ever heard of a phone?"

"I didn't want to risk waking you," she replied, echoing Reed's often-used excuse. She kicked off her high heels and padded into the kitchen. It'd been ages since she'd had an appetite like this.

Reed was right behind her. "You're actually enjoying this, aren't you? First you're late, then no phone call, then you throw my words back in my face. All right, I get the message."

"Message?" Megan turned away from the refrigerator she was peering into. "What message?"

"What's good for the goose is good for the gander. Isn't that the point you're trying to get across?"

"Reed, you know me better than that. I never try to score points. I was busy. It's as simple as that." Megan turned back toward the refrigerator. Lord, she was so hungry she could eat the proverbial horse. She pulled out the fixings for a sandwich and brought them to the table.

"Busy doing what?" Reed asked. He set a place for her, but his attention wasn't on his task. A piece of silverware dropped to the floor. Reed swore and substituted a fresh piece.

"Trying to get my old job back," she said calmly. She laid a generous supply of deli meat on her bread, then added lettuce and tomatoes.

"Trying to get your old job back?"

Megan scooped up a dollop of mustard with her knife. "Reed, would you stop repeating everything I say?" she requested. "I went back to the hospital to see about getting back my job on the children's ward."

"And?"

"Unfortunately they didn't have any openings."

Reed relaxed and sat down at the table. "Why didn't you say so in the first place?"

Megan didn't like seeing Reed's obvious relief. "I settled for another job, instead," she announced. "I'll be working the swing shift. In fact, I was able to start my training today. That's why I'm so late."

Megan remembered her interview at the personnel office. The woman in charge, Lynn Peerson, was an old friend of Megan's.

"Meggie, you know I hated to see you leave us," she'd said. "And you know I'd love to have you back. But there just aren't any openings in pediatrics right now."

"I'll take anything," Megan had said with desperation. "Anything."

Lynn flipped through her paperwork. "Well, we do have one opening," she said slowly, "but I don't know if you'd be interested. It's a trauma job, and it's only temporary."

"I've been trained in trauma nursing," Megan eagerly replied. "I had to be certified before I took that job in Africa, remember?"

Lynn nodded. "That's right, you did. But this job is the swing shift—three to eleven," Lynn warned. "I know your husband works days."

"That's no problem," Megan said in a determined voice.

"There's more. It's with the hospital's med-evac helicopter."

"Life Flight?" The Life Flight program had only been in the planning stages when Megan had resigned her earlier position.

"Yes. I don't know how you feel about flying with a trauma team. It's hard grueling work. There's a lot of action and a lot of stress."

"Did the last nurse suffer burnout?"

"No, she's in her final trimester of pregnancy. It was getting too hard for her to load and unload patients into the helicopter. She had to take maternity leave but should be back in about six weeks. That's why the position is open in the meantime."

Megan couldn't hide her excitement. Hard work was just what she needed. "I'm definitely interested, Lynn."

"Hmm." Lynn considered only a moment. "You'd need a training period to familiarize yourself with the helicopter's medical equipment. When can you start?"

Megan's eyes had gleamed with excitement. "Right now."

Reed's insistent voice brought Megan back to the present.

"I thought we decided you weren't going to work. You said we never have enough time together."

Megan poured herself a glass of milk, then rummaged in the cupboards for the potato chips. "And *you* said we'd spend more time together if I quit. Which we haven't. I'm tired of being home by myself."

She finally sat down and took a big bite of her sandwich.

"If you're working the swing shift I'll never see you!"

"You never see me now," Megan said between bites. How lovely to have an appetite again. "You're always gone."

"What would you have me do? Stay home all day? Become an aging playboy like my father? I despise that way of life."

Megan heard the anger in his voice. "I know that, Reed. And perhaps that's part of the reason you're so bored with me. I stay home all day and play the part of the useless wealthy wife. Like your mother."

Reed's face blanched. "You aren't useless, Megan. You and my mother are poles apart."

"Are we really? I wonder." Megan took a sip of milk, ignoring the hurt deep inside. The time for tears was past. It was time to face reality. "Perhaps a divorce is what you've wanted all along. Perhaps cutting me out of your life is your way of easing me into that possibility. Maybe you've even found yourself another woman."

"Megan, of course not!"

"I wish to God you had!" she flung back. "At least if there was another woman, I could understand why you avoid me."

Reed stood up, his hands tightly holding the edge of the table. "I've never heard you talk this way before, Megan. Never."

"That's because you're used to Megan the doormat. Megan, the adoring wife. Megan, the world's biggest fool." She picked up the second half of her sandwich. "She's gone, Reed. They're all gone. Meggie Mc-Cullough is back."

Reed straightened his chair back with awkward jerky motions. "You didn't file our marriage certificate, did you." It was a statement, not a question.

"No." She turned away from the pain in his eyes. She loved him, but she couldn't give in now. Megan knew one thing for certain. Even as a child, Reed had valued only what he'd earned with his own sweat. She had to make him value her the same way.

Her throat was tight with emotion. She reached for her milk, but Reed dashed it away with one savage swipe of his hand. The glass hurtled through the air, then exploded against the tile floor. Megan stared with wide eyes at the white splatters all over the cabinet doors.

"Jerry Davis is a dead man." His voice was terrible to hear. "If it takes every cent I have, I'll ruin him."

"Reed, you're such a fool!" Megan cried. She pushed herself to her feet and leaned over the table. "You don't understand! This isn't about you and Jerry. It's about you and me! *Me!* Just once can't you consider *my* feelings?"

Reed looked at her with disbelief. Then abruptly he turned and left the room, the sound of glass crunching under his shoes.

Megan forced herself to sit back down. She'd given up too many meals on account of Reed. This was one meal she intended to finish, and finish it she did.

Later she made her way to the bedroom, leaving the glass and spilled milk on the floor. Reed had made the mess. Reed could clean it up. But Reed was nowhere to be found. He wasn't in their bedroom, and after Megan had showered and climbed under the covers he still hadn't shown up.

She sighed heavily and turned out the light. The old Megan would have checked to see if his car was in the garage. The new Megan didn't. But either way, one thing remained unchanged. Megan was in bed alone, with only an aching heart to keep her company.

The next morning she was awake early. She didn't have to be at her training session until three, but she did have to buy a couple of new uniforms. The white dresses and slip-on nurses' shoes she wore on the pediatric wards were impractical for helicopter work. Lynn had given Megan the address of the local uniform shop that sold the one-piece jumpsuits and laced shoes Life Flight required its crew to wear.

Megan also planned to stop at the stylist's for a haircut. She's always worn her hair in a shoulder-length, easy-to-care-for pageboy until she'd stopped working. Then Reed had asked her to grow it long. She'd have no time for elaborate hairdos or her long manicured nails now. Both would have to go, and good riddance, Megan thought.

They were part of her old, useless life-style. Reed was right about one thing. She *wasn't* like his mother. The wealthy's privilege of staying home and doing nothing wasn't for her.

She climbed out of bed and slipped a robe over her naked body. She'd have a quick breakfast before getting dressed.

The kitchen floor and table were spotless, Megan saw. Reed must have cleaned up the mess sometime during the night. There was even a freshly brewed pot of coffee. Megan sniffed with appreciation and poured herself a cup.

"I'll have one, too, if you don't mind."

Megan whirled around in surprise. "Reed! I thought you'd be at work by now." She looked at his bare feet and chest, and his jeans. His hair was tousled, and he hadn't shaved. "Where have you been?"

"Down at the beach, walking."

Megan felt a pang in her heart. She and Reed always used to walk together. They both loved the ocean; that was why Reed had bought shoreline property in Malibu. But somehow those walks had dwindled in number, then finally disappeared altogether.

"I decided to take the day off," Reed said. He took the coffee she offered him and sat down.

"I hope you didn't on my account," Megan said worriedly.

"And if I did?"

"I hate to disappoint you, but I have to shop for new uniforms, get my hair done and run a few other errands."

"I could come with you," Reed offered.

"I'd like that." Megan smiled, then the smile faded. "But I'm meeting an old friend of mine for lunch."

"Jerry?" Reed asked with contained fury.

"No, Donna. She's a nurse. She and her husband, Bill, were always asking the two of us over." Megan put sugar in her coffee and slowly stirred it. "You never did get around to meeting her."

The accusation hung in the air.

"Anyway," she continued after a moment, "I'm getting back in touch with all my old friends. My plans are already made for the day, and I'm not going to break them. So if you want to go into work, go get changed," she said firmly.

Reed remained where he was. "It's been a long time since you and I had breakfast together."

"Yes, it has."

Megan popped two pieces of bread into the toaster. Reed stood up and moved behind her, his arms around her waist.

"It's been a long time since we've had a morning all to ourselves." His lips gently brushed against her neck, and Megan felt herself weakening.

"Reed, shouldn't you be getting in the shower?"

"Only if you come with me." Reed reached around and untied the belt of her robe. The sides parted, exposing her bare skin to his touch.

"I showered last night." Megan shivered as he pulled the robe down off her shoulders. His right hand gently caressed her breast, while the other traveled up and down a trim hip. "Reed, I know what you're trying to do, and it won't work."

He spun her around in his arms. Megan moaned at the contact of his naked chest with hers. His eyes glittered with triumph.

"Won't it, my love?"

Then he kissed her, hard and long and sweet. The kiss was Megan's undoing. They didn't make it to the bedroom. They didn't even make it to the living-room couch. Instead, their bodies came together on the plush rug before the cold fireplace, Megan urging him on with a passionate want that had them both trembling.

And despite the intensity of that wild, frantic joining, they both cried out—not words of desire, but words of love. Megan clung to him with a desperation that frightened her, afraid to let go, but knowing she must. Reed held her close, letting her choose her own time to pull free.

It almost seemed as if they could have remained that way forever. . . .

It was finally Megan who sat up, pushing at her hair. Reed grabbed her arm and pulled her back to him.

"No, Megan, stay."

She shook her head. "I've got to go."

"I can make you stay. I can have you begging me to love you again." The expression on his face was fierce. His hands tightened on her arms, imprisoning her. "You know I can."

Megan looked into the intimidating depths of his eyes and wasn't afraid. "You've always had my body. I've never wanted any man except you to touch me."

Reed's face lit up with victory. Megan knew he thought he'd won until she turned away from his kiss.

"But you don't have my heart, Reed—not anymore. If you want any chance of winning it back, you'll let me go."

Reed's hands instantly released her. The look on his face was one of total astonishment. For the very first time in their marriage, Megan had the upper hand.

She'd never thought it would hurt so much.

Five

"I can't believe what I'm seeing. Meggie McCullough, back at work."

The familiar voice startled Megan. She was out on the helipad, restocking the helicopter with medical supplies.

"I wish you wouldn't sneak up on me like that, Jerry," Megan said through the open window, but her warm smile took the sting from her words. Jerry was leaning on the perimeter fence. "What are you doing in this neck of the woods?"

"Hoping to take you to dinner. Your boss told me you eat at six-thirty, and it's almost that now."

Megan nodded. "Well, your timing is perfect. I'm done here. Just let me lock up." She reached into her jumpsuit for her keys, secured the medical supplies and drugs, and closed the helicopter's door. Then she opened the gate to the fence and gave Jerry a hug.

"I love your new look." Jerry took in the name tag, the digital pager that hung from her beige jumpsuit and the much shorter hair. "And I even get a hug, to boot. The old Meggie would have looked over her shoulder first to see if Reed was watching."

"You needn't sound so pleased with yourself," Megan replied tartly as Jerry took her arm. "This was all my doing, not yours."

"Yes, but I was the one who gave you the kick in the pants," he said smugly. "I deserve a reward."

"Or a jail sentence. I haven't made up my mind," Megan said, but she was still smiling. "Come on, the hospital cafeteria is in the basement. Believe it or not, they make a mean cheeseburger."

Once they were seated with their meals, Jerry studied her and said, "You look good, Meggie. You really do."

"I feel good—about myself, anyway. I'm working, and my life has a purpose again. It isn't pediatrics, but I like it. And it beats sitting at home waiting for Reed."

"How's Reed taking all this?" Jerry asked.

Megan dunked a french fry in catsup, considering. "I'm not sure. At first he was furious. Then he was positive he could change my mind. Now he's taking me seriously, at least for now."

"That's good, right?"

"I don't know. So far Reed's behavior has been perfect. Calls me like clockwork, keeps regular hours, waits on me hand and foot when I get home from work. And he hasn't mentioned my not filing the marriage license. Not once since the day he found out about it." Megan frowned. "Frankly, I'm waiting for the other shoe to drop."

"I see your point. Still, you can't blame the guy for trying. To be honest, I never thought Reed had it in him."

Megan shook her head. "Reed's been a model husband, but it's not the real Reed. I don't want him acting this way just because I'm threatening to leave him.

I want him to act this way because he thinks our marriage is important."

"In other words, you don't want to be married to a phony."

Megan winced at the words, but had to acknowledge their truth. "Something like that. I don't want Reed making a token effort. I have the sneaking suspicion that once that license is filed, he'll be right back to his old ways."

Jerry stabbed a french fry with a vengeance. "And making you miserable again."

"He doesn't mean to," Megan insisted. "And he has been awfully good to me these past couple of weeks."

"Perhaps, but I wouldn't be surprised if the true Reed Kendall shows up sooner or later. This performance of his can't last forever, and we both know it. You'll be right back where you started, trapped in a rotten marriage."

"I don't want that."

Jerry hesitated just a moment. "Then, Meggie, you may have to face the fact that your marriage is over."

"I can't!" Megan cried out in a voice so filled with pain it made a few heads swivel her way.

Jerry pushed aside his plate and reached for her hand. "Sweetheart, I'm sorry. You know I wouldn't hurt you for the world."

Megan pulled her hand away. "You're part of the reason I'm in this mess, Jerry. I wish I'd never invited you to my wedding!"

"I wish you hadn't, either. Watching the woman I love marry a man totally wrong for her..." Jerry's voice broke. He cleared his throat and started again. "Look, Meggie, there's a way to find out if Reed's serious about your marriage."

She lifted her head, her eyes wary.

"Tell Reed you've filed the license. Don't actually do it," he said. "Just *tell* him you have."

"You mean lie?" Megan said incredulously. "In all the time I've been married to Reed, I've never lied to him."

"I say now's a good time to start. It's an easy way to make the real Reed Kendall emerge," Jerry urged. "If he's a changed man, fine. If not, you can leave him with a minimum of fuss."

Megan cringed at the painful words, but continued listening.

"You know Reed will never give you a divorce. You can't afford all the smart lawyers he can. So save yourself a lot of heartache. Tell him you're now husband and wife, then sit back and watch his behavior. Who knows, maybe he'll continue being that model husband. If I had you for a wife, I know I would."

Megan felt her spirits rise. "Maybe you're right."

"I can't predict what Reed will do, Meggie," Jerry warned. "But at least this way you'll know for certain where you really stand."

Megan's expression was pensive. "I know where I stand. Reed loves me."

Jerry picked up his fork and reached for his pie. "Then, Meggie, you have nothing to fear."

Megan thought about Jerry's words during the drive home. She'd never lied to Reed before, and now she was going to. She couldn't deny feeling guilty and nervous, and yes, fearful. The moral implications of what she was about to do went against everything she believed in. Deceiving the man she loved was a contradiction of that very love.

But Jerry was correct about one thing. Reed would never agree to a divorce. And as much as it would hurt, Megan couldn't go back to the life she'd led before. If she stayed with Reed, she wouldn't have the strength to resist him. She knew herself too well. Leaving him would be the only chance for her to save Meggie Mc-Cullough from dying a slow lonely death.

She broke out in a sweat, and she rolled down the car window. The salty sea air wafted across her face, but tonight it didn't offer its familiar comfort. She checked her watch. It was after midnight. Reed would be waiting for her. He'd waited up every night since she'd started working again. She wondered how long that would last once he assumed they were married.

She shivered—but not from the night air.

Sure enough, the lights were on as Megan pulled into the driveway. Reed's voice greeted her as she stepped inside the door.

"Hi, sweetheart. Long day?" He took her purse and the bag with her soiled uniform, and handed her a drink.

"Thanks, Reed." She gave him a kiss on the cheek and took a grateful sip of the limeade. "Sorry I'm late, but we had a bad wreck on the interstate. We didn't get back to the hospital until after eleven."

"Was everything all right?" Reed asked as they both sat down on the couch.

Megan smiled at his concern. She remembered how interested he was in her work while in Africa. She'd often thought he would make an excellent nurse himself. He had a compassion and concern for the helpless that came straight from the heart.

"Yes. It was pretty hairy there for a while, but it looks as if our patient's going to be all right. We got to him in time."

"That makes all the difference," Reed said. "Perhaps I should look into getting a medical helicopter for the mine."

Megan shook her head. "No, it wouldn't be practical for you or your workers. The upkeep and medical staff would be wasted on all but the most serious traumatic injuries. And thanks to your safety policies, there aren't many of those. The aid station you have on the mine site and your clinic are more than adequate. I should know."

Reed nodded. "I'm glad. I'd hate to think I was neglecting my employees. Mining is a dangerous occupation. They deserve the best." He gave her a lopsided grin that had her heart doing somersaults. "However, so do you. I should know better than to bombard you with shoptalk the moment you walk in the door. That's probably the last thing you want to hear."

"Oh, no. I love talking to you about anything, anytime. I always have."

Reed edged a little closer and put his arm around her shoulders. "Do you still feel like talking?" he asked with a slight smile. "Or do you have any other... inclinations?"

Megan smiled back. She knew exactly what he had in mind. "I have those, too, Reed, but right now I'd like to go for a walk. I'm all keyed up from that last flight. It was touch and go for a while there with the patient, and I'm still too pumped up with adrenaline to sleep."

Reed kissed her gently on the lips, then lifted the glass out of her hand and placed it on the coffee table. "We can wait until later," he promised in a husky voice.

A few minutes later they were walking barefoot on the sand. The foam from the breakers hissed and splashed the bottoms of their jeans, while the breeze blew cool air over their bare arms.

"Cold?" Reed asked, his hand in hers.

"No, it feels good." Megan sighed with contentment, then turned toward Reed. The soft light from the full moon shone on his strong jaw and high cheekbones.

"You're a beautiful woman, Megan," Reed said as they continued their walk. "Even more beautiful when you're happy."

Megan let her smile speak for her. She was always happy when she was with Reed.

"I should never have neglected you," he said softly. "I guess I haven't been a very good husband."

Megan let go of his hand and put her arm around his waist. "Your parents' marriage didn't give you much of a role model," she said. "I had none at all growing up in a hospital. Neither one of us got much training for being married."

"Which we're not." Reed's voice held quiet reproach. "Are we, Megan?"

"I've always thought of you as my husband," Megan replied. "Whether the license is filed or not, that will never change."

Reed said nothing. They walked awhile in companionable silence, their arms tenderly locked around each other's waists. Megan wished it could always be like this, just the two of them. They were a good distance from the house before Reed spoke again.

"Shall we turn around?"

"Yes. I'm ready to go back."

"Perhaps tomorrow will be a little calmer for you at work."

"You never know. Some days we get as many as three or four calls and lots of emergencies. Other days we just sit around and do nothing. I hate that."

Reed looked at her with new understanding. "I imagine you do. You've had enough of that this past year, haven't you?"

"It's my own fault," Megan replied, not wanting to spoil the peace between them. "And my new job helps. I'm on the waiting list at work to get back into pediatric nursing. It might take me a year or so, but eventually I'll get there."

"You always did love children. I remember in Africa how they used to flock around you."

Megan laughed. "Only because I carried around pockets of candy, Reed, not because I was Earth Mother extraordinaire."

Reed shook his head. "It was more than just the candy those children loved. I realize that, even if you don't." A pause, then, "You've never talked about having your own children, Megan. Why?"

She hesitated and Reed instantly picked up on it.

"It's because of me, isn't it?"

"I know you'd make a good father, Reed," she said in a soft voice. "I keep waiting for your work schedule to clear up."

"In other words, you don't want to become a single parent," he said bluntly.

"I didn't say that."

"Don't deny it, Megan. We both know I'm never home."

Megan stopped walking and looped her arms around his neck. "You've been home lately. And your business hasn't fallen into the ground."

"No, it hasn't. I must admit the change has done us both good."

Megan rested her head on his chest. "Worlds of good," she echoed. She felt Reed's cheek rest atop her hair and let his love enclose her in a warm safe haven.

"So what are you doing tomorrow morning?" Reed asked, still holding her tight. "Do you think you'll have time for breakfast with your husband? Or lunch?"

"Oh, Reed, I can't," Megan moaned. She lifted her head, her eyes filled with disappointment. "I have to be at UCLA at eight."

"The university? Whatever for?"

"I have an appointment with a counselor to see about getting licensed as a nurse practitioner. I was finished with the required classes and only had to take the board certification exam..." Her voice drifted off. When she'd married Reed, her testing, along with everything else, was put on hold. It was a shame, considering she had everything she needed to be qualified. "I thought about taking some refresher classes first."

"You're going back to school?"

"Yes. I didn't get a chance to tell you. I'm sorry."

Reed put her slightly away from him. His actions were gentle, but Megan felt the tenseness in his body. "So when will you be attending classes?"

"In the mornings, with a practicum from noon till two."

"So you'll be gone all day at school, then working all evening?"

Megan heard the disapproval in his voice, but was unwilling to back down. "Since I was locked into the swing shift, it seemed like the perfect opportunity to register. I've always wanted to be a certified nurse practitioner. I could do so much more. I wish I'd been certified when I was in Africa. There never seemed to be enough doctors to go around. I want to be prepared in case that opportunity to help ever comes up again.''

Again silence fell between them. The waves continued to crash onto the shore while Megan waited for Reed to speak. Would he order her to give up her dreams again? Would she have to finally make a stand against the only man she'd ever loved?

''I guess you'll be pretty busy with both work and school. Let me know if there's anything I can do to help out,'' he replied.

Megan felt her knees buckle with relief. She discovered she was holding her breath and let it out on a long sigh.

''I'll be just fine,'' she managed to say. ''But thank you.''

''Well, we'd better get back to the house. You're going to need your sleep.''

But later in bed, Megan didn't sleep. She and Reed lay together in the most intimate of embraces. The pleasure and exquisite tenderness of his lovemaking had brought her to tears. Even now, after their passion was long spent, she was reluctant to close her eyes.

''Go to sleep, sweet Megan,'' Reed murmured, kissing her neck, ''or you'll never get up in the morning.''

''I hate to leave you, even to sleep.''

Reed cupped her face in his hands. ''Have I neglected you so much?'' he said, and Megan heard the self-condemnation in his tone. ''Close your eyes. I'll be here when you wake up in the morning.''

She gazed at him in mild disbelief.

Reed smiled. "Don't look at me like that. I promise. Now kiss me good-night. You have a lot to do tomorrow."

Megan took a deep breath. "I'll make sure I go to City Hall, too. I have some unfinished business to take care of."

"Oh, Megan, I do love you."

The look of joy and gratitude that Reed gave her took Megan's breath away. Then his lips and touch chased away fears. And for a second time that night, Megan postponed her rest.

Not that it mattered. Because long after Reed lay peacefully sleeping at her side, Megan was wide awake.

She'd never known how hard it was to sleep with a guilty conscience....

Six

Her feelings of guilt continued into the following week, for Reed was more attentive, more loving, than ever. He even took time off when the Life Flight helicopter was grounded with mechanical problems, and Megan found herself with an unexpected three days off.

"What are you going to do, Megan? Anything in particular?"

"Not really." She stretched luxuriously in bed. "Today's Friday. I don't have classes, and the hospital says we won't get the helicopter back until Monday."

Reed reached for her waist and pulled her closer to him. "I hate your working weekends. But since you're not going to work, I'm not, either. I have a surprise for you."

He sat up, the sheet falling from his bare chest, and reached toward the nightstand.

"Here."

Megan took the envelope he offered. "What's this?" she asked, puzzled. "Plane tickets?"

"I thought you might like to fly back East this weekend and see your family."

"Reed! Are you serious?" Megan flipped through the itinerary with excitement. "But we have to be at the airport in two hours. We'll never make it!"

"Calm down." Reed caught her as she would have jumped out of bed. "I packed for both of us last night while you were at work. All we have to do is throw on some clothes. The airport limo will pick us up in an hour."

"An hour?" Megan relaxed. "I can change in a fraction of that time." She wound her arms around his neck and said with a wicked grin. "What will I do in the meantime?"

Reed's eyes twinkled. "You could thank me for the tickets."

Megan was only too happy to oblige.

Her good mood continued throughout the plane ride. "I can't believe we're actually going home," she said. "It's been a long time. I haven't seen anyone since our..."

She faltered on the word, but Reed picked up the slack.

"Since our wedding. Hard to believe we've been married almost a year."

Megan shifted uneasily in her seat and looked out the plane's window, thinking of the license still locked in the bank.

"What shall we do for our anniversary?" he asked. "It's only three weeks away."

Megan put a smile on her face and turned away from the window. "What did you have in mind?"

"A huge bouquet of flowers, wildly extravagant gifts, a romantic dinner, or all of the above. Whatever makes you happy."

Megan considered carefully. "You know what I'd really like to do, Reed? Go back to Africa."

"Africa?" Reed was startled. "Megan, why? The living conditions at the mine aren't the stuff romantic anniversaries are made of."

"Oh, but, Reed, they are! We were so happy there. We worked hard, but we played hard, too. I didn't care that the bungalow was lucky to have running water. I didn't mind the heat, or the dirt, or any of that, because we were together. I have good memories of the time we spent there."

Reed gave her an assessing look. "You actually sound like you miss it."

"I do," Megan said simply. "I don't know why you won't take me with you on your business trips to the mine. I've asked you often enough."

"I thought you were just being polite. Most women wouldn't want to give up a comfortable home for a primitive bungalow in the middle of nowhere."

"I'm not most women, Reed. I really wanted to go," she said, hurt at all the opportunities they'd already missed.

Reed took her hand. His face was filled with regret and bewilderment. "Sometimes, Megan, I wonder if I really know you at all."

She managed a shaky smile. "I wonder the same thing about myself, sometimes. Perhaps we should compare notes."

Reed lovingly traced her cheek with his forefinger. "We'll do that in Africa, on our anniversary. We can have the flowers, gifts and romantic dinner there. Maybe this time you'll let me give you a necklace of Kendall diamonds."

"No, Reed. I have my engagement ring from you." She fingered the flawless stone on her finger. "That's the only thing I ever wanted. That, and you."

Reed shook his head with wonder. He leaned over and kissed her full on the mouth, oblivious of the other passengers. "Lucky man that I am, you've got me," he murmured.

Do I really? Megan wondered. *And for how long?*

But her outward appearance showed none of her anxiety. She maintained a calm and composed air until the plane landed and the taxi took them to her parents' home.

"Meggie, it's so good to see you again!" Mrs. McCullough embraced her daughter on the doorstep while Mr. McCullough shook Reed's hand. "What a surprise! I only wish you'd told us earlier."

"We had very little notice ourselves," Reed said. "Did we come at a bad time?"

"The rest of the family is out of town," Megan's father said. "Your great-great-uncle died, Megan, and everyone went to the funeral except us. We were going, too, but when we heard you were coming, we decided to stay home."

"I'm sorry, Dad. I didn't know."

Reed offered his condolences, but Mrs. McCullough dismissed his apologies for keeping them home.

"Don't apologize, Reed," she said. "Great-uncle Charles was a wise old man. He'd be the first to agree that the living come first. I wouldn't miss seeing you and Meggie for the world. The rest of the family can represent us at the funeral. Come on in. You must be starving."

Reed took Megan's arm, and the four of them walked inside. Despite the family death, dinner was a light-hearted affair.

"Married life must agree with you, Meggie," Mrs. McCullough observed. "You seem to be one of those fortunate women who sail through marriage."

"We've had our share of ups and downs," Reed said. "Most of which, I'm afraid, have been my fault. I haven't been a model husband, but I've turned over a new leaf."

"Don't be ridiculous," Mrs. McCullough scolded. "You must be doing something right. Megan looks so happy. She was such a sad little girl, you know."

"Mom, please," Megan said, but her mother ignored her embarrassment.

"It's true. She was very lonely in the hospital and desperate for attention. She'd do anything to get her father and me to stay a few extra minutes. I really used to worry about her. She was frantic when we'd leave."

"That was a long time ago, Mom. I'm fine now."

Megan concentrated on her meal, aware that all eyes were on her. She never liked to think about all those years alone in the hospital. The loneliness hurt far worse than the physical pain of her treatments. Even Jerry and the staff were a poor substitute for the family she loved.

"And your mother and I are both glad of it, Meggie. Sometimes I wonder if we did the right thing, leaving you all alone. Still, you seemed to get used to it."

I never got used to it. Not with you, not with Reed. But she couldn't ruin the meal by saying that. So she gave them a polite smile and took another mouthful of food. Her parents were fooled, but Reed wasn't.

Later that night in her parents' guest room, Reed brought up the subject again.

"Megan, I never realized how isolated your childhood was."

She stopped in the act of brushing her hair. "Why bring it up now? That's all in the past."

Reed unbuttoned his shirt. "Is it? You were alone so much in your youth. Maybe that's why you hate me working the way I do."

Megan felt a chill of foreboding run down her spine. She slowly replaced the brush on the vanity table and swiveled around to face him. "What are you saying, Reed? That I'm a clinging wife because of my lonely childhood?"

"I never said you were a clinging wife." Reed turned down the covers and sat on the edge of the bed to take off his shoes.

"You implied it."

Reed didn't deny the accusation. "You have to admit you hate being alone."

"What I hate," she said with slow-growing anger, "is your smug, totally erroneous armchair psychology."

"Megan, please—"

"Don't Megan me! You're making excuses for your behavior, as always. Most men work forty hours a week. You work easily twice that on a regular basis, and often more. Any woman would resent that, even one without my background. Yes, you've been around more these past couple of weeks—but how long will *that* last?" She shook her head. "You're not married to me, Reed. You're married to your job! I might as well be single for all I see of you!"

"You knew I had a career when you agreed to marry me," Reed said irritably. "I've told you time and time again I have no intention of becoming like my father."

"I am sick to death of you using your father as an excuse!" Megan retorted. "But since you brought him up, let me say that you're more like him than you know.''

Reed rose to his feet, his fists clenched. "The hell I am!"

Megan's eyes narrowed. "You are! You give me money, instead of your time, like him. You give me gifts, instead of giving me yourself, like him. You live in your own little world that holds no room for a wife. You even have your own mistress like your father, only you prefer an office to warm flesh. You don't know how to be a good husband any more than he did. As far as I'm concerned, you're a regular chip off the old block!"

Reed sprang forward. He grabbed her arms and jerked her to her feet. "How dare you? I love you, Megan! My father never loved anyone except himself. He never took care of his wife."

Megan met his gaze head on. "Neither have you! You've put me on a pedestal and left me there! I don't want to be loved from afar, Reed! I'm a flesh-and-blood woman. I want my husband's arms around me. I want children at my feet. Lord knows I've prayed for them often enough."

Her lips twisted bitterly. "I'll be lucky if I ever conceive. On the rare occasions you do bother to make love to me, you usually have ulterior motives, like wanting me to quit work, or to file our marriage license. My God, Reed, how do you think that makes me feel?"

It took Reed a moment to answer. When he did, his voice was bitter. "Considering your low opinion of me, Megan, I'm surprised you even bothered to file that license."

Megan yanked her arms free. "I didn't!"

Reed's face blanched. They both stood frozen for seemingly endless minutes. Megan wished herself dead a hundred times over for putting that awful look on his face.

It was a while before he was able to say, "You lied?" The words were choked and strangled. "You lied to me, Megan?"

"Yes," Megan whispered. "Like you lied to me. You promised until death do us part." She shook her head, tears filling her eyes. "But you left me a long, long time ago."

Megan sank into the chair and buried her face in her hands. She couldn't bear to look at Reed any longer. She closed her eyes and fought her tears. Reed hated to see her cry. She wouldn't make things any worse for him than she already had.

It didn't matter. When she looked up, Reed was gone.

Seven

He left a note of apology for her parents, saying he was flying to New York on business. As Kendall Diamonds had another branch there, Megan's parents were understanding. Megan was all too painfully aware that no note was left for her.

Now she was desperate to get back home. She planned to cut her weekend short, but that was not to be. The rest of her family returned from the funeral and weren't about to let her leave. As it was, Megan barely made her scheduled flight. Everyone kept pressing her to stay.

Only the fact that she had to be back at work convinced them to let her go.

"Don't be such a stranger," her mother said when kissing her goodbye. "You and Reed come again real soon."

Megan nearly broke down and wept. She didn't even know where Reed was.

Once at the airport, she immediately checked with the ticket agent. When she heard Reed had cashed in his ticket for an earlier flight home, she felt a little better. Megan desperately wanted to see him and apologize. Not for what she'd said about their marriage—for those words had been too long unspoken—but for breaking her promise.

I want you to be faithful. Utterly loyal. No lies. I won't marry you without that promise, Reed had said when he'd proposed to her.

Megan had given him her solemn vow. Yet she'd broken it by listening to Jerry Davis and lying to Reed. That was a grave error, and one she intended to rectify. She could hardly wait for the plane to touch down at Los Angeles International. The cab ride home seemed to take forever, and Megan's nerves were practically in shreds by the time they finally reached the house.

She hurriedly paid the driver and raced inside.

"Reed?" she called. "Reed, are you home?"

Only silence greeted her. Megan dropped purse and suitcase on the floor and hurried through the house. There was no sign of him. A check of the garage revealed that his car was gone. His suitcase wasn't in the storage room, either.

Megan slumped with disappointment. It was late Sunday night. Why wasn't he home?

On a sudden impulse she called his office. The answering service picked up.

"No, Mrs. Kendall. Your husband isn't working today. He's not expected back until tomorrow."

"Thank you." Megan hung up numbly. She busied herself with unpacking and getting her things ready for the morning. She'd have a full day with both class and work.

She could only hope she'd be well rested. She didn't think she'd get much sleep wondering where Reed was. No matter how much practice she had going to bed alone, she never got used to it.

Never.

Three days later Reed still hadn't appeared or called, neither at home nor at the office. She had a hard time concentrating in class and had to force herself to stay alert at work. Finally in desperation she called Jerry.

"No, I haven't heard from Reed. He's left you?" Jerry asked with barely controlled anger.

"I . . . I don't know," Megan said miserably. "That's what I'm trying to find out."

"Stay put, Meggie. I'm on my way over."

Megan counted the minutes until Jerry arrived. She was at the door waiting to let him in the moment he pulled into the driveway.

"Oh, Jerry, thanks for coming. I'm sorry to bother you so late at night, but I had to talk to somebody."

"I'm not worried about me. I'm worried about you. Meggie, what's going on? Where's Reed?"

Megan sat down on the couch, her face the picture of despair. "I wish I knew."

"Tell me what happened." Jerry sat down next to her. "I thought you said Reed was on his best behavior."

"He was. We even flew to my parents' home on Friday."

"Talk about once in a blue moon." Jerry was incredulous. "Reed actually took you to see your family?"

"Yes. Things were going so well. Reed arranged everything. We were supposed to spend the whole weekend there, but—" Megan broke off abruptly.

Jerry took her hands in his. "But what, Meggie?"

"He accused me of being a clinging wife. . . ."

"That'd be quite a trick, since he's never home to cling to," Jerry said angrily. "Go on."

"I got really angry and said some things I shouldn't have."

"Like?"

"I told him I'd lied about filing the marriage license. He got up and left. He didn't stay one night at my parents'. He didn't even say goodbye." Her voice broke. "I haven't seen him since."

"Oh, Meggie, I'm sorry. I wish there was something I could do."

Jerry put his arms around her and held her tight. Megan rested her head on the shoulder of her dearest friend, taking the comfort he offered, but wishing more than anything that it was Reed's arms around her, Reed's voice whispering in her ear.

She sat quietly for a long time until a familiar voice reached her ears.

"Well, isn't this a touching scene."

Megan jerked her head up, her pulse quickening with excitement.

"I should have known it wouldn't take you long to show up on my doorstep, Davis." Reed's voice was diamond-hard. "But then, you have a nasty habit of showing up when you're least wanted. Starting with my wedding."

Jerry flushed an angry red. "I was invited. Just like I was invited here."

"Not by me, you weren't." Reed's eyes glittered with anger. "You've been a thorn in my side since the day Megan chose me over you. I've put up with it because you're Megan's friend, but I'll be damned if I will any longer."

He grabbed Jerry's arm and yanked him to his feet. "Get away from my wife! And get out of my house before I throw you out!"

"And leave Megan with you? Not that it would be very long, considering your track record. How could you abandon her?"

Jerry shook himself free and tried to get back to Megan. Reed immediately stepped in front of her, effectively blocking Jerry's way.

"Stop it, you two! I won't have you fighting!" She placed a soothing hand on Reed's shoulder, but he refused to be calmed.

"I walk into my own home and find my wife in the arms of another man. What do you expect me to do, Megan? Offer to fix him a drink?"

"Please don't be angry, Reed. I was frantic for news about you. Jerry knew I was upset."

"So naturally he had to race over here and comfort you. What did you have planned next, Jerry? As if I couldn't guess."

"Reed! You know Jerry and I aren't...wouldn't..." Her words trailed off.

"Only because you won't allow it. Jerry would have you in bed in a second if it were up to him. It wouldn't even matter to him that you're married. Isn't that right, Jerry?"

Jerry's face grew even redder. "But thanks to me, Meggie's *not*, is she?" he retorted.

Reed's fists clenched, and Megan threw her arms around him, trapping his arms at his sides.

"Jerry, please go," she begged. "This is our business—mine and Reed's."

"Not anymore," Jerry spat out. "You made it my business when you used my safe-deposit box to store your wedding license."

Reed pushed Megan's hands away and turned toward her in furious shock.

"You made it my business when you agreed to my plan," Jerry continued.

"Plan?" Reed's voice was hoarse. "What plan, Megan?"

"*My* plan," Jerry announced. "Meggie was going to file your license, but she didn't trust you. So I advised her to keep it locked up, pretend she'd filed it, and then wait and see." His expression was smug. "She didn't have to wait long, did she? You walked out on her without even so much as a goodbye."

Reed's expression was terrible to see. "Lying to me was his idea, Megan? Not yours?"

"Yes." Her answer was a bare whisper. "Reed, I'm sorry."

"Sorry? You involved him in our marriage, you let him influence you, and you're sorry? Megan, couldn't you even keep this between the two of us? Do you trust me so little?"

Megan dropped her eyes in shame, unable to meet his gaze. "Please," she begged. "I did what I thought was right."

"You did what *Jerry* thought was right—right for him. Not for us."

Reed looked at her as though she was a stranger. "I'm going out," he said in a tight voice. "When I get back, I want him gone. See to it."

"Reed, wait. Don't go! Reed, come back!" She made to go after him, but Jerry got to her before she could reach the door.

"Let me go, Jerry!" Megan frantically tried to escape his embrace. "I have to go after him."

"He doesn't want you, Meggie! Don't you see that? But I do, damn it. I do!"

Megan tried to turn away from Jerry's kiss, but he wouldn't let her. His lips met hers with all the hunger Reed's did, but there was one big difference. Megan always responded to Reed. Jerry's kiss did nothing for her. After a moment, Jerry realized what Megan had always known.

"It's not there between us, is it?"

Megan wiped at her mouth with a trembling hand. "There was never an 'us.' All we had was our friendship. And if I've lost Reed because of you, we won't even have that."

"Meggie, you don't mean it!"

"I'm serious, Jerry. I was never more serious in my life. Now I want you to leave. Please don't come here again."

"Don't say that," he pleaded.

Megan backed away from him when he would have taken her in his arms once more. "Go home, Jerry."

Jerry's face turned an angry red. "I'll go—for now. But I'll be back. Because your sad excuse for a marriage isn't *my* fault. It's Reed's."

Megan watched Jerry leave. As the door closed behind him, she said sadly, "And mine, Jerry. And mine."

She was sitting quietly on the couch when Reed returned. He looked at her, but said nothing. Instead, he went to the bar and poured himself a drink.

"Where were you?" she asked.

"Out on the beach, taking a walk." His lips twisted in irony. "I seem to be doing a lot of walking lately."

"No, I mean over the weekend. Did you really go to New York?"

"Yes." He sat down on the bar stool, leaving the drink untouched. "I figured I might as well salvage something of the weekend. I took care of some things in my New York office, then flew home immediately after."

"Always business. Even in the midst of all this." Megan sighed.

"Not just business, Megan. I did some thinking, too." He stared out into the distance at the waves breaking beyond the huge bay window, his expression unreadable. "You're right about one thing. We don't have much of a marriage. Maybe we should call it quits."

Megan felt her heart contract and her veins turn to ice. "You can't mean that!"

"We make each other miserable, Megan. Tonight's just another example."

"That was my fault," Megan said. She hurried to Reed's side. "I should never have lied to you."

"It's not just the lie, Megan. It's not even the license being unfiled. It's much worse than that. I never set out to make you unhappy. Believe it or not, I thought we had a good marriage. We might not have been together much, but I always knew you were there for me." He gave her a bittersweet smile. "At least, I thought you were. I was happy, and I foolishly thought you were, too."

"Reed—"

"It appears I've been living under a delusion." He finally lifted his glass. "Here's to reality."

"We'll just try harder." Megan reached for him, but he deliberately avoided her touch.

"At what? A marriage that doesn't exist, either on paper or in actuality? No."

His answer was stark and unyielding, and Megan felt fear grip her heart.

"It's time to face facts. License or not, our marriage is over."

"It isn't! Reed, you have to believe me—this isn't what I wanted when I didn't file our license!"

"What *did* you want, Megan?"

She fought hard for control. "I wanted to wake you up. I wanted you to see how things really were."

"You did that, Megan. You did that."

A terrible silence descended. Reed stared at his drink while Megan damned herself for not filing the license the day Jerry mailed it to her. She'd only hurt herself, and worst of all, she'd hurt Reed. It was a long time before she could bring herself to speak again.

"What now, Reed? What do we do now?"

"What most unhappy couples do. You go your way and I'll go mine."

"You mean split up?" Megan said in an anguished voice.

Reed nodded once, as if not trusting himself to speak.

Megan picked up her purse. She withdrew her checkbook and savings-account passbook with trembling hands, then walked over to the bar and laid them down in front of Reed. Then she removed her house key from her key ring and placed that before him, too.

He looked up, confused. "What's this?"

"I'm the one who should leave. Everything here belongs to you." She hesitated. "I hope you'll let me keep my car. I know you paid for it, but I need some way to get to work." She bravely pushed the pile toward him.

Reed covered her hand with his. "No, Megan. What's mine has always been yours. Besides, this house has been your home more than it's ever been mine. I'll go."

Megan felt hope at his touch. "Reed, you don't have to. I don't *want* you to," she said desperately. "I love you."

He gently pulled his hand away from hers. "And I love you. But it seems, Megan, that isn't enough."

He rose to his feet, leaving his unfinished drink on the bar. "I'll be at the office if you need me for anything. I don't want you to worry about money. I'll take care of things, as always."

"Damn it, Reed, I never worried about money or *things*. All I ever wanted you to take care of was *me!*"

"Then give Jerry Davis a call. I'm sure he'll be willing to oblige."

His words wounded deeply, and Megan was filled with sorrow, knowing that was his intention.

"Goodbye, Megan. I hope you find what you're looking for."

Megan's cry, "But I already have!," went unheeded. She was alone.

Eight

Megan never knew how she survived that awful night when Reed packed his bags and left. She never knew how she made it through those terrible days afterward, realizing he wasn't coming back.

Thank goodness for her job and her classes. She threw herself into work with a vengeance, hoping to wear herself out so she wouldn't lie awake at night. She accomplished the former, but not the latter. Megan couldn't sleep in the big empty bed she'd shared with Reed. Memories of the past and futile wishes for the future tormented her.

Finally in desperation she started sleeping on the couch. At least there she could snatch a few hours of rest to get her through the day.

From Reed, she heard nothing. Money was automatically deposited in her bank account, and the household bills were paid through Reed's office. The few times Reed needed to communicate with her, it was done through Barbara. When Megan tried to reach Reed, Barbara insisted she leave a message.

"I'm sorry, Mrs. Kendall," Barbara apologized. "But I have my orders. He isn't to be disturbed."

"By anyone, or just by me?"

There was an embarrassed silence on the other end of the line, and Megan knew she had her answer. She defiantly drove to Reed's building in downtown Los Angeles. The security guards were apologetic, but refused her entrance.

"I'm sorry, Mrs. Kendall. We have our orders."

Megan had proudly held back the tears and left. What she'd always feared had finally happened. Reed had cut her out of his life completely.

She didn't try to contact him again.

"Megan, you have to accept the fact that Reed doesn't want you," Jerry told her one afternoon as they walked along the beach. Despite her wishes, he had started stopping by on a regular basis, and Megan was too lonely to send him away. "You don't eat, you don't sleep. You've got to get your mind off him."

She couldn't deny his words. There were dark circles under her eyes, and her appetite had all but disappeared.

"If you're not careful, you're going to make yourself sick."

"I'm not." She lifted her chin with pride. "I'm doing quite well, thank you. I have class and my job, and I keep busy."

"Too busy, if you ask me." Jerry reached for her arm and stopped her progress across the sand. "Doesn't your replacement at the hospital come back in a few weeks?"

Megan frowned at the thought. "Yes."

"What will you do then?"

"I don't know. There still aren't any openings in pediatrics. I checked."

"Perhaps that's a good thing. You need some time to get over this. You should take a nice long rest."

Megan pulled her arm away and stared out over the water. "I don't want to rest," she said with irritation. "I've had enough of that to last me a lifetime."

"Meggie, don't be angry. I shouldn't have said rest. I should have said honeymoon."

Megan stared at him in amazement. "With whom? Reed?"

"No, damn it! With me!"

"You?"

"Yes! I can give you everything you want from a man. Love, companionship, children. We can even work together. I have a good practice in pediatrics. The two of us could make it even better."

Megan was unable to take in his words. "You can't be serious."

"I'm more serious than I've ever been about anything in my life. Just think, Meggie, the two of us together again. Happy again, like before you met Reed."

"Jerry, haven't you listened to anything I've said these past few weeks? We had some good times. But I don't love you. Not like that."

"Meggie, we've loved each other since we were children. We've shared so much! First the hospital where we grew up, and now our profession. We have so much in common to build on. Let's not throw that away."

Megan shook her head. "I love Reed. I'll always love Reed," she said simply.

"After the way he treated you?" Jerry's voice rose in frustration. "After all the mistakes he's made?"

"I've made some, too," Megan replied slowly. "And the biggest one I made in our marriage was listening to you. The only thing Reed ever asked from me was loyalty. I let him down."

She watched the water foam white over her feet, then recede again. "I can never forgive myself for that."

"He doesn't love you like I do!"

Megan met her friend's tortured gaze and gave him a sad smile. "Even if that was true, it doesn't matter. I want Reed. I can't—I won't—settle for anyone else."

"Even if it means spending the rest of your life alone?" Jerry asked hoarsely.

Megan's eyes took in the waves as they broke onto the shoreline. "When I was in the hospital all those years, I thought being alone—being without anyone's physical presence—was the worst thing in the world. I was wrong. The worst thing is knowing the people you love don't care."

"Meggie—"

"As long as I knew Reed loved me, I was never really alone. Only I was too stupid to realize it." Megan's voice broke and she closed her eyes.

Jerry tried to put his arms around her for comfort, but Megan shook her head. Her grief was too personal to share with anyone—except the one man she'd driven away.

Jerry stood by awkwardly. Megan wished he would leave.

"What will you do, Meggie?"

She took a long shuddering breath. "I don't know. Pray for a miracle, I guess."

Jerry awkwardly patted her shoulder. "I'm sorry. I never meant to make you unhappy."

She managed to give him a tiny smile before she turned and headed for the house. "It's not your fault, Jerry. It never was."

Much to her relief, he didn't follow her. She watched as he drove away. Megan had the place to herself, along with the familiar pangs of loneliness. She stared at the phone, willing it to ring and be Reed. Suddenly she couldn't stand it any longer. She had to get away from the house before she went crazy.

She grabbed her car keys and purse and headed for the front door. Her life wasn't over, she told herself. And her marriage wasn't over yet, either. She still had almost two weeks before her anniversary—plenty of time in which to legally become Mrs. Reed Kendall.

Megan traveled the route that would take her to the bank. She'd leave the safe-deposit key with a clerk for Jerry to collect and file the marriage license today. If Reed really didn't want to be married to her, he'd have a court fight on his hands. She wasn't going to make things easy for him.

Megan smiled to herself as she retrieved the license. Reed had fallen in love with her once. If she asked for his forgiveness, he might fall in love with her again, given the chance. And in the meantime, Megan would show him that she could wait—alone—as long as necessary.

"My goodness, but isn't this a bit late to be presented for filing?" The elderly clerk at City Hall peered at the date on the license, then removed his bifocals. "What in the world took you so long?"

Megan decided nothing but the truth would suffice. "An old friend was best man at my wedding. He took it upon himself to hide this because he thought I'd picked the wrong man."

The clerk gave Megan a look of confusion. "Did you?"

"No," Megan said fiercely. "That's why I'm here. Would you please file this and give me a copy for my records?"

The clerk put his glasses back on, then nodded. "I expect your husband was pretty upset when he heard."

Megan felt the familiar pain stab at her heart but offered the clerk a brave smile. "I'm trying to set things straight," she managed.

The clerk returned her smile. "You wait here, ma'am. This may take a little longer than usual, but I'll have you proper and legal yet."

A half hour later Megan left City Hall with a validated marriage license in her purse. There was a sense of rightness about being Reed's wife, a sense of contentment. Her next stop was the hospital's personnel office.

"Megan, what are you doing here?" Lynn asked. "Isn't today your day off?"

"Yes, it is. I wanted to see when my last day of work is with Life Flight."

"I don't even need to check my files for that. You have just two more weeks left, Megan, if you want it."

"If I want it?"

Lynn nodded. "The woman you replaced is ready to come back from maternity leave sooner than she expected. But I told her you probably wanted to finish out the original assignment, as we haven't had any other openings come up for you."

"I need to talk to you about that," Megan said. "I want you to take me off the waiting list."

"Off the waiting list? Are you going back to school full-time? Or have you found other employment?" Lynn asked with dismay.

"Neither. I've finished my classes. I'm going back to Africa."

"To work for your husband's company again?"

"Actually, I hadn't considered that, though it's a definite possibility," Megan said thoughtfully. "Our anniversary is in two weeks, and I—we—wanted to spend it where we first met. If my replacement is eager to come back to work, I'm willing to step aside."

"Let me call her. I can let you know right now," Lynn said, picking up the phone.

A few minutes later it was official. Megan was free to leave.

"How long are you going to be gone?" Lynn asked. "I'm sure an opening will come up here sooner or later. We can always use good nurses like you."

"So can my husband's clinic," Megan said firmly. "Thanks, Lynn, but I think I'm going to get my old job back."

Lynn smiled at Megan's enthusiasm. "That shouldn't be too hard. You *are* the boss's wife."

Megan rose from her chair and nodded. Yes, she was the boss's wife. And she intended to take full advantage of that....

Back home, she dialed the long-distance operator and soon had her husband's African clinic on the line.

"We could certainly use you back here, Mrs. Kendall," the clinic director said. "We've had a terrible flu epidemic, and we're shorthanded. Both the miners and my staff have been hit hard."

"I'm on my way," Megan said. "Have personnel put me back on the clinic staff. I'll let you know my travel arrangements so someone can pick me up."

"Very good, Mrs. Kendall." To Megan's relief, he didn't question her authority at all. "Shall we expect Mr. Kendall, too?"

"No, he'll be tied up with business here in Los Angeles for quite some time," Megan replied, not actually knowing, but guessing it was the truth. "It'll be just me on the plane."

"We'll look forward to seeing you, then. Goodbye."

She hung up. It was all too easy, really. She'd just have to pack a few things, forward her mail, buy herself a plane ticket—and wait for Reed.

She knew he would come. He regularly kept tabs on the mine and his business. Megan was positive she'd seen him more at the clinic than she ever had here in town. She would win him back then. She knew it.

She reached for her bag and withdrew her marriage license. She debated sending it to Reed in the mail, then changed her mind. If Reed wasn't taking her phone calls, who knows what he might have instructed Barbara to do with any mail from her.

There weren't any pushy secretaries or apologetic security guards at the clinic. Reed couldn't avoid her there when he went to check on his men. The license would go with her, Megan decided. She would give it to Reed in person. She owed him that.

Besides, Megan had another reason for wanting to see Reed face-to-face.

She was pregnant.

Nine

The fans in the Kendall Diamond Mines clinic whirled at full speed, but they only moved the hot night air around. Nothing could dissipate the heat.

"How many more patients do we have waiting outside?" Megan asked, wiping a sweaty brow with the back of one hand. The flu epidemic was still in full force, and everyone had been working overtime.

"None for you," the head doctor said firmly. "You've been here since sunrise, and it's dark now. Go home, Mrs. Kendall. Get some rest."

"I don't mind staying," she argued.

"And I don't want your husband breathing down my neck if you get sick yourself. Please, for my peace of mind, go to your bungalow."

Megan frowned but did as she was told. Ordinarily she hated getting special treatment because she was the boss's wife. However, if truth be told, the thought of a meal and getting off her feet held a lot of appeal. The only negative aspect of her pregnancy had been a nagging fatigue. As she knew that was perfectly normal and rest was the only cure, she didn't argue further.

"I'll see you all tomorrow," she called out.

Already the staff was busy with the next patient. So much for being indispensable, Megan thought. Still, she was satisfied with her day's work. The gratitude of the patients was touching. It made her feel as though she'd accomplished something, even if her feet did ache and her once-pristine uniform was soiled.

She'd take a long cool shower before eating, she decided. Then she'd fix herself dinner. Despite missing Reed, she was hungry these days. She was careful to take good care of herself. She'd wanted children for so long she was determined to give Reed's child a good start in life.

That's odd, Megan thought. *I didn't leave any lights on in the bungalow.* She hurried to her door and stepped inside.

"Reed!" Megan cried out with joy. She'd hoped and prayed for him so long it was hard to believe he was actually here. And when his arms wrapped around her, she thought she was in paradise. It wasn't until she heard his angry voice that she came back to reality.

"Megan, where have you been? I've been worried sick."

"I..." She looked at her uniform, then back up at him. "I'm working at the clinic."

"All this time?"

"I know it's late, but—"

"I mean the past two weeks, Megan! Have you been here for the past two weeks?"

"Yes. Didn't you know?"

"Of course not! I thought you were in Los Angeles." Reed ran a hand through his hair with agitation. "I've been looking for you all this time. I still have people looking for you back home."

Megan's disappointment was acute. "You didn't come out here because of me?"

"How the hell was I supposed to know you were in Africa? For all I know you could have been kidnapped. Even Jerry didn't know where you were."

"You checked with Jerry?"

"Of course I did! I was concerned, Megan! You could have told me!"

"How?" Megan returned his accusation with one of her own. "You wouldn't take my calls, and your guards wouldn't let me in the building. What did you expect me to do, Reed? Hire a skywriter?"

Reed flushed at her sarcasm.

"I'm sorry, Megan. I was angry. I never thought you'd actually leave town."

"No, you wouldn't. Even at our worst, you always expect me to be quietly waiting for you." Megan took the opportunity to pull away from his embrace. She sank onto the room's tiny couch with none of her customary grace. "My job with Life Flight was only temporary, and there weren't any openings at the hospital. I needed something new, so I put myself back on the payroll out here."

"You put yourself back on the payroll?" he echoed.

"It wasn't hard. I am the boss's wife, after all, and no one thought to question me. Or you, it appears. I'm sorry you were worried, Reed. You didn't have to search any farther for me than your latest personnel records. You used to take it upon yourself to personally meet each new employee, remember?"

There was silence, and Megan knew Reed was recalling the first time they'd met.

"Besides needing a job," she went on, "I needed to get away from Jerry. Coming here took care of that, too."

Reed continued to stand. Megan studied him carefully, suddenly aware of the dark shadows under his eyes, the tautness of the skin over his cheekbones and the stubble of beard on his chin.

"Jerry was frantic when I told him you were missing," he said. "Both of us thought the worst. Why didn't you at least let *him* know you were coming here?"

Megan took off her shoes and tucked her bare feet under her. "I didn't want him following me. Jerry's wreaked enough havoc with my life. Two years ago I came to Africa to get away from him. I should have stayed away," she said emphatically.

"Because he loves you? Or because—" Reed's voice grew hoarse "—you love him?"

"No, because I *don't* love him, and I can't convince him of that. No matter what happens between us, Jerry's going to have to let me go. I only have room for one man in my heart." She looked up at Reed, her eyes filled with love. "Jerry Davis isn't that man. He wants more from me than I'm willing to give. He always has. And when I give him a little, it costs me dear." Megan swallowed hard, unable to go on.

Reed came and sat down next to her. "Like what happened to us?" he quietly asked.

She nodded, her eyes closed with pain.

Reed took her hands in his. "I once asked you for your loyalty, Megan. Your actions may not have shown it lately, but deep down I know you've always been true."

She opened her eyes with surprise—and with the first faint glimmering of hope.

"I came back to the house—back to you—only to find you gone. Megan, I went crazy. I went tearing over to the hospital and then the university. No one knew where you were," he said in a tortured voice. "Not even Jerry."

"But Reed, I told Lynn—"

"Lynn who?"

"Lynn Peerson. She works in personnel at the hospital. She knew I was coming back here. I didn't keep it a secret."

"Damn! She wasn't in the office when I was. I talked to a man who said you'd left, and your name had been taken off the waiting list for any other jobs. He couldn't give me any more information. I didn't know what to think, what to do."

Megan tentatively laid a hand on his shoulder, hoping she wouldn't be rebuffed. "I'm sorry you were worried, Reed. You know I'm a sensible woman—well, most of the time," she corrected.

"All of the time," Reed said. He gathered her close, much to her delight. "Megan, I've been so foolish. You were right."

"About what?"

"About me giving you everything except myself." His eyes were dark, haunted. "My father never shared anything without a price tag. I thought being a good husband meant giving you whatever you wanted, no strings attached."

"But, Reed, all I ever wanted was you! I didn't want your money and what it could buy."

"I've had a lot of time to think lately, and I finally figured that out. But when I went to you, you'd gone. Oh, Megan, I thought it was too late for us."

She felt a shudder run through his body and held him close. "So you hired people to find me?"

"Yes. And I came here."

She was puzzled. "On business?"

"*Personal* business. Tomorrow is our anniversary. You said you wanted to spend it in Africa. I was desperately hoping you'd show up."

Joy flooded her heart. "And I was hoping *you'd* show up. I wanted that more than anything in the world."

She kissed him with all the love and devotion in her soul. And when Reed kissed her back, again and again, it wasn't his usual kiss of all-consuming passion. It held a new, deeper intimacy that welcomed her back and promised a future for both of them.

"Reed, I've made so many mistakes. Can you ever forgive me?"

"Forgive you? I've been the guilty party here."

Megan shook her head. "Not the only one. I've been a clinging wife, just like you said. I realized it after you left. When I was a child in the hospital, I was denied my family's presence—their physical presence. I felt abandoned and unloved."

"And when I was gone so much you felt those same old fears?" Reed said with compassion.

"Yes. I never realized until lately that when someone loves you, you're never alone. I've been so stupid." She laid her head on his shoulder, smiling when he kissed her hair.

"I think we've both been a little short on sense, Meggie."

Megan sat bolt upright. "Reed! You called me Meggie!"

"Yes. Do you mind?"

Megan thought about that. The way Reed said her name had always made her feel special. "My family calls me Meggie, and so do my friends. You're the only one who calls me Megan." She gave him a loving look. "I think I'd like to keep it that way."

"As long as you decide to keep *me*," Reed said fiercely.

"Just you try to have it any other way." Megan nestled against him.

They sat entwined together in silence, aware of each other in the most acute sense, yet comfortable enough to stay still.

A whistle blew outside, signaling the end of the shift.

"It's eleven o'clock," Reed said with obvious surprise.

Megan nodded. "Do you realize that in another hour it's our anniversary? Oh, yes," she said when Reed would have spoken. "It's official. I filed our license with City Hall before I came here, and I have the copy to prove it. To quote the old clerk who waited on me, we're 'proper and legal' now."

The look on Reed's face, then his tight embrace, took Megan's breath away.

"Reed, let go! I can't breathe."

He relaxed his hold but didn't release her. "I was planning on jumping through hoops to get you to marry me again, my love. I want you for my wife. I want you as the mother of my children. I never dreamed . . ."

Reed's kiss this time left Megan trembling with desire.

"Reed," she said in a shaky voice, "let's go to bed. Now."

He stroked her face gently. "Let's wait until it's officially our anniversary. You need a shower and, I suspect, a good meal. Why don't you clean up while I fix us something to eat?"

Megan sighed, then asked hesitantly, "Reed? Did you mean what you said?"

"About what, my love?"

"About children. Do you really want them? Will you make time for them?"

"Them, *and* you," he solemnly assured her. "I swear it, Megan."

She smiled and rose to her feet. "There's a casserole in the refrigerator. Just heat it up. I'll be back before dinner's ready," she promised, giving him a kiss on the forehead.

"Take your time." Reed grinned. "We have all night."

Megan nodded, her heart finally at rest. As she stepped into the shower, she ran her hand over the slight swell of her stomach. She wondered if Reed would be able to guess she was pregnant. Probably not, she thought. She wasn't very far along. She'd have to tell him later.

But not on their anniversary, she decided. Not tonight. Tonight was just for her and Reed. She shivered with joyous anticipation. If only she didn't have to bother with eating. She hoped Reed wasn't making a big fuss in the kitchen.

He wasn't. The casserole was heating quickly on top of the stove. He kept a watchful eye on it while waiting for his overseas call to go through. Finally it did.

"Hello?"

"It's Kendall," Reed said bluntly. "She's here."

Jerry Davis exhaled on a slow breath of air. "Thank God. Is she okay?"

"Yes. Megan came to Africa to celebrate our anniversary, just like we planned. She filed our marriage certificate, Davis."

There was a moment's silence on the other end. Then, "She's really all right?"

"Yes. We both are."

"I appreciate your calling me," Jerry said. "I know you didn't have to."

"You're Megan's friend. And except for that damn license, Davis, you've played fair. I'll grant you that."

"I won't next time," Jerry said fervently. "If you make Meggie unhappy again, I'll be back."

"There won't be a next time." The conviction in Reed's voice rang true. "Ever."

When Jerry spoke again, even Reed winced at the pain in the other man's voice. "Send Meggie my best."

"I will." A pause. Then, "Davis?"

"Yeah?"

Reed hesitated just a moment. "Thanks." With that, he hung up. For a long time he stood motionless, his fingers still around the receiver. It wasn't until the casserole started to bubble and steam that he regained his composure.

When Megan emerged from her shower, Reed was stirring their dinner with easy strokes.

Megan sniffed appreciatively over his shoulder. "Almost ready?" she asked.

Reed ignored the question. "I love you, Megan." He reached for her and tucked her under his chin. He held her tight with one arm and continued to stir with the other. "I'm the luckiest man alive."

Megan's pulse quickened at the look in his eyes.

"Forget the dinner." She took the spoon from his hand and tossed it into the sink. Her eyes were bright and shining as she turned to face her husband. "Everything's really going to be all right, isn't it."

It was a statement, not a question. Reed smiled, guided her lips to his and answered her, anyway.

"It is, my love." He kissed her once, kissed her twice, then kissed her again. "Happy anniversary, Megan."

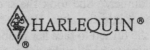

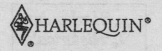

HARLEQUIN®

MARRIAGE BY Design

Harlequin proudly presents four stories about *convenient* but not *conventional* reasons for marriage:

- ♦ To save your godchildren from a "wicked stepmother"

- ♦ To help out your eccentric aunt—and her sexy business partner

- ♦ To bring an old man happiness by making him a grandfather

- ♦ To escape from a ghostly existence and become a real woman

Marriage By Design—four brand-new stories by four of Harlequin's most popular authors:

CATHY GILLEN THACKER
JASMINE CRESSWELL
GLENDA SANDERS
MARGARET CHITTENDEN

Don't miss this exciting collection of stories about marriages of convenience. Available in April, wherever Harlequin books are sold.

Harlequin® Historical

LOOK TO THE PAST FOR
FUTURE FUN AND EXCITEMENT!

The past the Harlequin Historical way, that is. 1994 is going to be a
banner year for us, so here's a preview of what to expect:

* The continuation of our bigger book program, with titles such as
Across Time by Nina Beaumont, *Defy the Eagle* by Lynn Bartlett and
Unicorn Bride by Claire Delacroix.

* A 1994 March Madness promotion featuring four titles by
promising new authors Gayle Wilson, Cheryl St. John, Madris Dupree
and Emily French.

* Brand-new in-line series: DESTINY'S WOMEN by Merline Lovelace
and HIGHLANDER by Ruth Langan; and new chapters in old favorites,
such as the SPARHAWK saga by Miranda Jarrett and the WARRIOR
series by Margaret Moore.

* *Promised Brides,* an exciting brand-new anthology with stories by
Mary Jo Putney, Kristin James and Julie Tetel.

* Our perennial favorite, the Christmas anthology, this year featuring
Patricia Gardner Evans, Kathleen Eagle, Elaine Barbieri and
Margaret Moore.

**Watch for these programs and titles wherever
Harlequin Historicals are sold.**

HARLEQUIN HISTORICALS...
A TOUCH OF MAGIC!

HHPROMO94